MOVING TO YOU

PJ FIALA

ROLLING THUNDER PUBLISHING

MOVING TO YOU

by P.J. Fiala
January 2016

OTHER TITLES BY PJ FIALA

CONNECT WITH PJ

Reader's Club
PJ on Facebook
Tweet PJ
See inspiration photos on Pinterest
Goodreads

COPYRIGHT

Printed in the United States of America
First published 2016
Fiala, PJ
Moving to You / PJ Fiala
p. cm.
1. Romance—Fiction. 2. Romance—Suspense. 3. Romance - Military
I. Title – Moving to You

ISBN-13: 978-1-942618-21-8
ISBN-10: 1-942618-21-2

DEDICATION

I've had so many wonderful people come into my life and I want you all to know how much I appreciate it. From each and every reader who takes the time out of their days to read my stories and leave reviews, thank you.

My critique partner, Brenda, thank you so much for your help and support. I'm truly blessed to have found you.

My beta readers, Terri, Anita, Danni, Barbara, and Kimberly, ladies thank you so very much for your suggestions, praise and time.

Of course, my editor and proofreader, Mitzi and Marisa, thank you ladies.

Last but not least, my family for the love and sacrifices they have made and continue to make to help me achieve this dream, especially my husband and best friend, Gene. Words can never express how much you mean to me.

To our veterans and current serving members of our armed forces and police departments, thank you ladies and gentlemen for your hard work and sacrifices; it's with gratitude and thankfulness that I mention you in this forward.

1

Lost in thought as he flew down the highway, the heat was oppressive in the high nineties; the scenery had changed from the desert of the Badlands to the lushness of Custer about an hour ago. The fragrance of pine and freshly-cut trees mixed with the heated blacktop and the occasional odor of road kill kept JT alert. What kept him awake was thinking of the design of the next motorcycle he wanted to build. He was determined to make his dad realize what a great bike designer he was. Sure, he was good at sales —no one questioned that—but that didn't mean he always wanted to be in sales. He wanted to design bikes—full-time. He wanted to fabricate parts and bend metal to his liking and pound out a gas tank that looked totally different than any they had seen. His dad was proud of the bike he'd built for this Sturgis Build-Off. Now, if they could win first place and cement that idea in his dad's head, life would be good. Hell, even top three would be fucking great.

Pulling into Shady Pines—a quaint little town just outside of Custer—and rolling down the main street, a smile stretched across his face. One of the things he loved most about this town was the old western feel of the buildings. You could sit and dream of being a cowboy strutting along the sidewalk, entering a saloon and ordering up a pint. As they drove just out of town, the older buildings turned into a park, and then an auto garage about a mile down from that.

Looking up ahead, he saw Porcupine Road. Turning his right signal on, JT floated over to the right and turned into the mostly gravel parking lot of OK Leathers Saloon. Damn gravel parking lot meant their bikes were going to be filthy when they finally got to the house they were renting.

JT, his brother Ryder and his dad, Jeremiah—or Dog, as most folks called him—had known Oakes for years. His dad had served in Iraq with Oakes. Just before Rolling Thunder Motorcycles opened, Dog, JT, and Ryder had built a bike for the Sturgis Build-Off—it was their first—and brought it out here. They didn't win, but they learned a lot about what people were looking for. That's when JT fell in love with building. He walked around for hours looking at all the bikes and designs and asking questions. Ah, the excitement was hard to contain. Over the past three days on the ride out here, his skin practically itched with the anticipation of getting here and showing off his new design. It was more exciting than the first time, because this time, it was all his.

Dropping the kickstand and dismounting from his bike, JT stretched and bent from the waist to relieve the stiffness from sitting on his bike for so long. His brother, Gunnar, and Gunnar's fiancée, Emma, pulled in and parked alongside him; Ryder and his fiancée, Molly, pulled in next to them. A few of the Rolling Thunder crew were riding along this week and each found a spot in the parking lot. Dog was driving the truck pulling the fifth wheel and another trailer with JT's show beauty and some of the other bikes for those riding in the fifth wheel.

Turning to look at the front of OK Leathers, JT noticed instantly that it needed a coat of paint. The worn and weathered boards showed a hint here and there of the bright red color that used to grace its front entrance. Though battered and worn, the front door was solid wood and oddly adorned with a fresh coat of light gray paint. The front decking on the building and the Pergola over the picnic tables were built of sturdy logs, and little lights hung between the rafters of the overhang. Each picnic table had a mason jar sitting on it, half filled with tiny stones of varying colors and a bright flower peeked out of the top of the jar, its stem firmly pushed in the stones. JT smiled, looking at the contrast between the front of the building and the cheeriness of the picnic tables. Ceiling fans hung in the Pergola, slowly rotating, creating a slight breeze—just enough to keep the stifling heat from sucking your breath away.

"I hope to God there's air conditioning and gallons of beer in there," Gunnar said as he slapped JT on the back. Holding Emma's hand, Gunnar pulled her through the gray door and disappeared into the bar.

"It looks a bit run-down, doesn't it?" Ryder stopped alongside JT and looked at the front of the bar.

"Yeah. I remember it being a place I couldn't wait to get to each evening after we left Sturgis. But it looks like no one comes here anymore. Even now, the parking lot only had two bikes and one truck before we got here."

Molly smiled. "Times change, and sometimes people don't change with the times. Let's go see what's going on. I'm anxious to meet with bigger-than-life Oakes Leathers." Molly pulled Ryder's hand, urging him inside.

JT pulled the bandana off his forehead and unwrapped it. He removed the rubber band from his ponytail and shook out his long blond hair. He spent a bit of time rubbing his scalp, then finger combing his hair back before wrapping the rubber band around his new ponytail. Shaking the road grime from the bandana, he rolled it back up and tightened it around his head. He looked back at the truck and fifth wheel and saw his dad and stepmom, Joci, walking toward him, along with some of the Rolling Thunder employees.

As he stepped up to JT, Dog said, "She looks a little different than the last time we saw her."

"Yeah. Let's go see how Oakes is fairing."

Stepping into the bar, the cool air flowed over him, instantly lowering his body temp. A sigh escaped his lips as the smell of fresh grilled burgers and French fries from the lunch hour teased his nose.

A gravely barking laugh rang out. "Dog, goddamn, it's good to see you."

A large man, around six foot two inches and two hundred twenty pounds came walking around from behind the bar. He grabbed Dog in an aggressive hug, slapped him on the back a few times and held him at arm's length.

"Damn! Marriage looks good on you."

Dog laughed and reached for Joci, pulling her close. "That it does. I'd like to introduce you to the woman who puts the smile on my face. Joci, this is Oakes."

"Pleased to meet you, Oakes." Joci's gray eyes crinkled at the edges as her smile creased her face and her dimples came out to wink at him.

"Ooowee would you look at her? Damn, girl, you're a beauty." Oakes grabbed Joci in a hug and gently patted her on the back.

Joci squeezed Oakes hard and laughed at his enthusiasm. "Thank you. I think I'm going to enjoy spending time here with you."

Oakes laughed, and for the first time, looked around at the folks gathered close. Reaching forward, he wrapped his arms around Ryder. "Good to see you, boy. You've grown. What's it been, six years or so?"

Ryder laughed returning the hug. "Good to see you, too, Oakes. I guess it's been about that long." Looking back at Molly, he pulled her forward. "Oakes, this is my fiancée, Molly. Molly, Oakes Leathers."

Oakes shook Molly's hand as his broad face split in a smile. His face hadn't been shaved in at least three days, but his grin was infectious and his graying hair was trimmed short and neat. Oakes let out a whistle as he looked into Molly's sparkling blue eyes. The blush creeping into her cheeks mixed with the redness from the heat they had just left brightened her face further.

Oakes looked around and Gunnar stepped forward, holding his hand out to shake Oakes'. "I'm Gunnar, Joci's son."

"Our son," Dog quickly added.

Gunnar smiled and nodded at his dad. "It's nice to meet you,

Gunnar. Your dad told me about you after he and Joci married. Congratulations on joining the Sheppard family. It's a good one."

"Yes, sir, I agree. Nice to meet you, as well." Gunnar grasped Emma's hand, kissed her fingers and said, "This is my fiancée, Emma."

Oakes smiled brightly as he shook her hand.

JT stepped through the circle of people. As soon as Oakes saw him, he stepped up and wrapped him in a fierce hug. He slapped him on the back a few times, then stood back. "Good to see you, boy. I'm excited as hell you're all here."

JT genuinely smiled at Oakes. "It's great to see you, too. I can't wait to bend your ear about some bike designs."

In the past, Oakes and JT would talk about different designs and some of the bikes Oakes saw living out here near Sturgis each year. He got pictures when he could and they would talk about the craziness some of these bikers could come up with.

"Grandpa, tell them you know me." A beautiful little girl with long blonde, wavy hair was tugging on Oakes' jeans. Oakes looked down at her and quickly scooped her up, loudly kissing her cheek. Laughing, he looked at Dog and Joci. "This is my granddaughter, Dakota. Dakota, these are my friends from Green Bay, Wisconsin." Holding his hand out toward Dog and Joci, Oakes continued, "They have a little baby now and her name is Madison."

"Oh, can I see her? I love babies." Dakota smiled and craned her neck around the group to see who might be holding a baby.

Joci giggled. "She's at home with her grandma and grandpa and several aunts and uncles. Maybe we'll be able to bring her to meet you next time."

Dakota's smiled turned to a cute little pout as she said, "Okay."

"Oakes, you didn't tell me how beautiful she is." Dog smiled at Dakota and she laughed. She wrapped her little arms around Oakes' neck and kissed his cheek.

Turning to walk behind the bar, Oakes said, "Let's get you all something to drink." He pulled a bar stool up to the inside of the bar, at the end next to the wall and gently set Dakota on the stool. "You have your books, Kota?"

Nodding her blonde head, Dakota pulled her pink sparkly backpack off the bar and reached in for her books. Oakes smiled at his granddaughter and started pulling beers from the coolers.

JT watched Dakota quietly reading in the corner. The denim skirt she wore covered the top half of her legs, and her red cowboy boots swung back and forth in time to the music playing on the juke box. The light blue t-shirt she wore had a red pony on it. It wouldn't be long before his baby sister, Maddy, was her age. He pulled up a stool at the end of the bar nearest to her, and she looked up and smiled at him.

"You gonna stay at Grandpa's house?"

"Yep. Where do you live?"

Dakota looked at her Grandpa to see if she could say anything. Oakes smiled and said, "He's good people, honey."

Dakota nodded. "I live over the garage with Momma."

"Over the garage? The one out back?" JT's brows furrowed.

"Yep. Momma and Grandpa fixed it up. It's great. I have a pink bedroom and Momma has a coral one. What color is your bedroom?"

JT laughed. "My room is blue. My mom helped me paint it."

Dakota looked down the bar. "Which one's your momma?"

JT pointed next to him, where Joci sat watching the two of them converse. "This is my mom. Where's yours?"

Dakota looked at Joci for a few moments and burst into a giggle. "You don't look like your momma, but I look exactly like mine. Everybody says so." Her beautiful hazel eyes, framed with thick lashes showed intelligence. She spoke with a maturity that didn't seem to fit her tiny body.

JT laughed. "I look like my dad. Everybody says so." His grin widened as he waited for her to respond. She looked just past Joci at Dog and then she giggled. She nodded once and said, "Yep." She set her book aside and turned on her stool so she was facing JT. "My mom went for a ride. When Rog calls, he makes her mad; she needs a minute and she takes her bike out for a ride."

Oakes heard her comments and walked down the bar to Dakota. "Kota, honey, did Mommy talk to Rog today?"

"Yep. She was mad and told him not to call her every time he gets in trouble; she don't want to hear it."

"Doesn't. She doesn't want to hear it," Oakes gently corrected her.

"Oh. Yeah. She doesn't want to hear it."

Oakes smiled at her. "Do your studies, honey."

Dakota picked up her book and opened it up on her lap.

Oakes turned and caught Dog's gaze. He rolled his eyes and went to serve another beer to one of the Rolling Thunder guys.

2

Kayden's lips were tight as she flew down the road. When would she finally be rid of that jackass? When? He promised to leave her alone; she'd won her court case removing him as one of Dakota's legal parents, but, still, that son of a bitch kept on dogging her. Now, he might go to jail again, and what does he do? He calls her! What is she supposed to do about it? Dammit, that guy will be the death of her.

She navigated the corner with ease. Her hair flew behind her, snarling up in the wind, and her tank top was little protection from the harsh rays of the sun or the road if she dumped it. But, at the moment, this bit of freedom was what Kayden needed. Nothing cleared her head or brought her back to earth like a bike ride. Thank God she didn't sell it when she'd needed the money. She almost did, but her dad talked her into keeping it. He must have known she needed this.

Turning into the back of the parking lot, behind the garage where she lived above, Kayden reached forward and pushed the button fastened to her windshield to open the garage door. As she waited for it to open, she looked to her right and saw that the parking lot was full. Dad was expecting guests from Green Bay today; it was all he had talked about for the past two months. She had cleaned the house all day—the one their guests would be renting and living in for the next two weeks. Dakota helped her, following her around the house with her little dust rag as Kayden cleaned and scrubbed and polished all the furniture and counters to a shine. It gave her time to dream about some of the work on her clothing designs she still needed to complete before tomorrow. It would be a late night for sure.

The house was perfect, and Kayden and Dakota had a great day getting all the little snacks ready for their guests. She did a little extra shopping at her dad's urging; he wanted Dog and the crew to enjoy themselves and the house. There were six bedrooms—big ones, at that—two living areas, a big kitchen and dining room and five bathrooms, all ready for them. The bar in the basement had been recently refinished and the wooden top shined and sported unopened bags of nuts and jars of jerky and a refrigerator full of beer. She didn't want to add the beer; she wanted them to come down to OK Leathers and spend money. But Oakes insisted. She hoped she and Dakota would be able to live in the house one of these days, but right now, it helped them pay the bills.

She pulled her bike into the garage and closed the door. As she walked to the bar, she fingered the tangles from her hair as much as she could. She glanced down at her clothing, she hadn't gotten too dirty today, her white tank top only had one little smudge on it. It'd have to do.

Walking in from the back door through the kitchen, Kayden stepped out behind the bar and glanced at their patrons.

"Mommy!" Dakota yelled as she scrambled off her stool and ran to her. As Kayden scooped her up, she smiled into her daughter's face and kissed her forehead.

"Were you good for Grandpa?"

"Yep. And I made some new friends."

Kayden laughed. Of course, she did; the little girl's friendliness was infectious. She could talk to a wall and enjoy herself. She set

Dakota down and the little girl grabbed Kayden's hand and pulled her down to the end of the bar.

"JT, this is my momma. See? She looks like me."

∼

J T looked at Kayden. His stomach flipped and gooseflesh rose on his arms. The woman standing before him was stunning. Taller than his future sisters-in-law, she was around five foot five and slender. She wore a white tank top that showed off her breasts and they were...spectacular. Tight jeans hugged her hips and legs and made her look leggy and delicious. Her long brown hair was messy, but cascading down her back, giving her the look of a model. But the wary look on her face said *hands off*. Her smile, forced but dazzling, showed the hint of a dimple on the right side. Her hazel eyes were unusual, green in the light of the bar, but as she leaned forward to shake JT's hand they turned to brown.

"Nice to meet you, JT. I'm Kayden." JT shook her hand; its softness such a contrast to his roughness.

"Nice to meet you, as well," JT managed to say, but his throat was suddenly dry.

A silence followed as they looked at each other and then Dakota interrupted, "Staring isn't nice. You told me I can't stare."

Instant heat flamed up Kayden's body, her cheeks burning from color. She looked down at Dakota. "I wasn't staring, and it isn't nice."

Chuckling, Dog stood up and offered his hand across the bar. "Dog, and this is my wife, Joci."

Introductions were made down the bar. Kayden came back to Joci and Dog and said, "I've been to the house and cleaned it all up for you. There are snacks and, should you decide to cook, most basic spices and condiments are up there. Daddy had me fill the fridge with beer, and I've left our cell phone numbers on the counter if you need anything or have any questions. If you need me to come up and show you how to use the air conditioner or anything else, just give me a call. It's only about a mile from here."

Reaching into her back pocket, Kayden pulled a key and piece of paper out and laid them on the bar in front of Dog and Joci. JT watched her reach back, which showed him a slight view of side boob. Crap, that swelled his manhood up further. Her smile was genuine when she looked at Joci, and she was gorgeous. Her lips were full but not overly so. Her teeth were perfect and straight and then she talked. Shit, she had her tongue pierced. Damn. She bent slightly to grab a glass from under the bar and filled it with ice. Using the soda gun, she poured herself a glass of white soda. That's when he saw an inscription tattooed on the inside of her wrist. He couldn't read it, but it was there—something to explore later.

JT took a drink from his beer bottle and glanced over at Dakota. She was watching him; her little book lay open on her lap like she was reading, but she wasn't. That little girl was smart, watching everything. When he set his bottle down, he smiled at her and winked. Her lips spread open in a big smile. She wiggled her little red cowboy boots back and forth and shrugged her shoulders. She glanced at her mom, who was watching JT.

Oakes walked up to Kayden and softly said, "You okay? I heard you spoke to Rog today."

Kayden's mouth formed a frown. She slid a gaze over to Dakota and raised her eyebrows. That girl listened to everything.

"Yeah. He's probably going to jail again, which is good, so I won't have to worry about him not heeding the Court's Order regarding his custody—or lack of custody. But, I wish he'd stop calling me—period. It stresses me out."

"What did he do this time?"

Kayden let out a long breath. "Robbery. Again. This time it's armed robbery."

"Stop taking his calls, Kayd. You've gotten rid of him, and he's out of both of your lives; leave it be."

"I didn't look at my phone before I answered. Kota and I were coming home from cleaning the house when he called. I grabbed the phone and answered."

3

Wiping the bar down after the Rolling Thunder group left, Kayden mused about them—nice family, little drama, or so it seemed. They were a large group, each of them tired, and none of them seemed crabby or irritable. Then, there was JT. He made her tingle—everywhere. Might be fun to play with him while he's in town. She hadn't had a good romp in a long damn time. There was something about a man with a long mane of hair, and he had a ruggedness about him she liked. The sex would be smoldering and then he'd go home. No attachments. Yeah, nice.

The back door opened, then slapped closed. Kayden sighed; she'd been meaning to ease that spring for weeks now. Dakota was going to get pinched in that door or knocked over in some way. She'd have to put it on her very long list of stuff to get done around here. First, the painting needed to be finished.

Kayden tossed the rag into the hamper under the bar and stacked the coasters neatly on the rail. "Jess, the order came in this morning and I've put the fresh hamburger on the top shelf for you." Kayden swiped her hands on the side of her jeans and headed to the kitchen.

Rounding the doorway and skirting the prep counter, she wandered to the back door, thinking Jessie needed help carrying in supplies. As she walked past the built-in grill and stainless steel prep counter, she halted in her tracks.

"What are you doing here, Boon?"

Boon was big, brawny, gnarly, and nasty. His hair was snarled and it usually looked like he didn't own a comb. He wore a blue bandana tied around his head, shouting "Dakota Devils." Go figure. It was the only MC that went so far as to pound their chests with their own doo rags. He leaned against the far wall next to the back door, arms crossed, showing off the full sleeves in which skulls and crossbones seemed to be the common themes, though there was no rhyme or reason. He'd get drunk and have one of the members tattoo him. Idiot.

"I came to see if you were taking care of my bar," he drawled out, nice and slow as if she were stupid.

Kayden crossed her arms, facing him. "This is MY bar, not yours, and you have no business being in here. And you're not allowed in the kitchen."

He sneered and gave off what she supposed was a laugh, though it sounded like a growl. "You'll sell this bar to me, Kayden Leathers, at the price I want. We've done a good job of running your Goody-Two-Shoes business away; you won't be able to hang on to this much longer. Now that Rog's going to jail, you'll be dealing with me."

Trying to keep her voice steady and not show any signs of fear, she said, "I'm not dealing with anyone. The bar is not for sale, and you aren't buying it. Now get out before this gets real nasty."

Her heart was hammering in her chest. She hated this guy and he scared her. He looked at her as if he would like to devour her, and she hated that, too. Mostly, she hated the Dakota Devils and every member, including her ex, Rog.

Boon pushed himself off the wall and slowly took two steps toward her. She held her ground. He reached out and pinched her chin between his thumb and forefinger. "We'll see," he ground out. Leaning forward, he tucked his nose into the crook of her neck and inhaled deeply. He leaned back, looked into her eyes and threateningly said, "Love the smell of fresh pussy."

The sound of a bullet entering a chamber made him freeze. "Get your filthy hands off my daughter, and get your disgusting ass out of MY bar or we can have you transported by ambulance. Your call."

Boon turned and looked into the very angry eyes of Oakes Leathers. Oakes was about an inch taller than Boon, and sturdy for an old guy. Now in his fifties, Oakes was still broad, and his hair had completely grayed out in the past few years. Lines around his eyes told the true story of a hard life and worry. The front of his shirt was covered in sweat and his face was red. But, there was no mistaking it; he'd hurt anyone who touched his daughter and granddaughter. That was going to make things a little harder for the Devils with Rog out of the picture.

Holding his hands in the air, Boon smiled at Oakes. "Easy, old man. I'd hate to have your finger slip on the trigger."

"Then you'd better not give me cause to twitch. Get out." Oakes' eyes slightly squinted, showing Boon there was no argument to be had. Boon slowly walked toward the door, opened it and stepped out, keeping his eyes on Oakes.

As soon as he stepped out, Oakes walked to the screen door and watched Boon get on his bike and drive away. He turned to Kayden. "You okay?"

She rubbed her forehead with the pads of her fingers. "Yeah. Hate that guy. All of them."

"I know, darlin'." Removing the bullet from the chamber of his Ruger 9mm, Oakes pocketed the pistol in his waistband holster. He started toward the front of the bar. "Where's Dakota?"

"She's in the apartment changing into her swimming suit with Payton and the kids. They're going to the pool today."

Payton, Kayden's best friend since high school, had two little ones of her own. Catcher was seven and looked just like his daddy with his dark hair and eyes. Ruby was the same age as Dakota and looked like her momma, having short blonde hair and blue eyes. The kids were cute and well-behaved and Dakota loved spending time with them. Payton's husband, Duncan, worked for the state park system as a ranger, and this time of the year, he worked long hours. Payton took Dakota in the afternoons while Kayden worked in the bar.

"Okay. You okay while I finish scraping the rest of the paint from the east side of the bar?"

"Daddy, let me do that. You stay inside where it's cooler. I don't want you having another heart attack." Her brows furrowed and her mouth turned down. She worried constantly about her father. It'd be nice if he worried about himself a bit.

"I've got it, Kayd. You've done all of the outside except for the east side. I want Dog and the crew to see it painted before they leave town."

Kayden put her hands on her hips. "Why? Why do you care about them so much?"

Oakes pulled a bandana from his back pocket, swabbed his face and neck, and clumsily stuffed it back in. "I want him to see this place as it used to be, not as it is now. Dog's built one of the finest bike shops in the country. They have people coming to them from all over to build their bikes. On top of that, he holds an annual Veteran's Ride for a local veteran each year. He's good, his boys are good, and I'm proud to know him. I was proud to serve with him during a war. He's my brother, and I want him to be proud of me, too."

Sighing heavily, Kayden responded, "We'll get this place back, Daddy. We just have to find a way to keep the Devils from ruining the rest of our business."

Oakes nodded once and turned to grab a bottled water from the refrigerator. "I'll be done in about an hour, girl. Get ready for the dinner hour. Dog and the crew are coming back down. They wanted to clean up and rest a bit. I want to finish scraping and then shower before they get here."

4

Stepping out of the shower, JT grabbed the towel from the counter. Opting to stay in the basement bedroom, next to the newly-remodeled bar area, he figured he could come and go without having to slog through the house. He wanted to stay in the fifth wheel, but some of the employees who joined them had asked to stay out there. Dog parked it on a level patch of grass, close enough to the fire pit so they could sit under the awning and watch the fire. The new fifth wheel slept eight, allowing them plenty of room. Great accommodations, and it didn't cost them anything. After all, it wouldn't feel like much of a vacation if you stayed in the same house as your boss.

Tossing the towel into a corner, he stepped into the bedroom and pulled a clean pair of boxer briefs from his duffle bag. Sliding them up and giving himself a couple of tugs, he flopped down on the bed, staring at the ceiling. He was tired, but he was also wired. What was it about Kayden that struck him so? Since leaving the bar, all he thought about was getting back there. She was compelling in so many ways. Those eyes of hers had the ability to change color depending on the light. He bet when she had an orgasm, they'd change again. He wanted to see that for himself.

ly about
that. He bet she looked sexy as fuck straddling it, her long legs on the
footboards, her breasts swaying and moving with the feel of the road.
They looked spectacular in the tank top she wore today—more than
a handful. Mostly what called to him was her wariness. She wasn't
coming on to him like it was business as usual; she seemed almost
shy or sad—maybe a combination of both. And, now, he had a raging
hard-on and no one to take care of it but himself. Figured.

Feeling like he was going stir crazy, JT sprang from the bed,
pulled a green Rolling Thunder t-shirt out of the drawer and slipped
it over his head. Grabbing jeans from his duffle bag, he quickly
dressed. He stepped back into the bathroom and dragged a brush
through his still-damp hair and tied it at his nape. He decided to
forego the shaving. He'd been thinking about growing a beard—a
Vandyke or something—maybe he'd get a good start on it while he
was here.

He stepped out of the bedroom into the television room where he
grabbed a beer from the fridge. The remote to the large flat screen
was laying on the bar, so he turned it on and looked around the room.
It was fantastic. Definitely something he'd want his game room to
look like when he got around to remodeling. For now, his house was
just fine; after all, it was just him there. Glancing at the bar, he
noticed the top was shiny and smooth. Several layers of glaze had
brought out the natural colors of the wood's grain. The beauty of the
grain and knots added a fabulous interest to the otherwise plain bar.
He stepped back and looked at the rest of the room. Basic carpeting,
theater chairs—six of them—all facing the television and a pool
table. Behind the bar, the freshly-polished oak cabinets completed
the total look. The decorations on the wall were antique metal gears
and handles, probably from an old wood mill in the area. He
wondered if Kayden had decorated it. He shook his head and slugged
down his beer and tossed the bottle in the recycle bin.

"JT?"

He walked around the bar and stopped at the bottom step to look
up at his dad. "Yeah?"

"You ready to go soon? I assume you're coming with us to eat at Oakes'." Dog looked down the stairs at JT and furrowed his brow. "You okay?"

"Yeah. I guess I'm just feeling restless. I'm going to go for a ride, and then I'll meet you there."

"Okay. We're just waiting for the girls to get ready." Dog chuckled.

JT shook his head. "Yeah. I'll meet you there."

Grabbing a clean bandana from his drawer, JT tied it around his head and stepped outside to his bike. They had all parked under the upper deck to help keep the bikes from getting wet if it rained. The ground looked dry as could be, and they'd stirred up clouds of dust driving down the gravel road. But, it was a shelter. He navigated the steep gravel driveway and onto the road, taking his time down the mile-long gravel. At the end where the gravel met the main drag through Shady Pines and off to the left was where OK Leathers stood. As he neared, JT saw Oakes outside scraping paint off the side of the bar. He stopped and waited for the traffic to go by and watched Oakes. The man looked beet red. Dog had mentioned that Oakes had a heart attack.

"What the fuck are you doing, old man?" JT muttered.

Shaking his head, JT pulled into the parking lot. Dismounting, he walked toward Oakes; JT could hear him breathing heavily. Then he noticed Oakes had stopped moving; he was leaning against the wall.

"Oakes? Are you okay?" JT's brows furrowed as he sped up to reach the older man's side. As he stood in front of Oakes, he saw the bright red skin coated with a layer of sweat, the front of his shirt was soaked from sweating, and his chest was rising and falling alarmingly fast.

Oakes looked at him, almost as if he didn't recognize him. After a few beats, he closed his eyes, then slowly opened them again. "JT. I'll be right in; I just needed a bit of a rest."

"I think it's more than that. What in the hell are you doing out here? It's still in the nineties, and you shouldn't be doing this type of work with your heart condition."

Oakes reached out a big rough hand and grabbed JT's muscled

arm. "You can't say anything to Kayden. Not to your dad either. Nothing."

"I don't know what I would say. You're working yourself to death? You're not doing well? What?"

Oakes released JT's arm and with a shaky hand he reached over for the lawn chair sitting against the wall. Flopping into the chair with a grunt, he tilted his head back and closed his eyes. JT reached down and grabbed the bottle of water sitting on the ground and handed it to Oakes. Bringing it to his lips, Oakes took a drink and waited for it to refresh him.

"Oakes, did you scrape this whole building?" JT stepped back and looked at the front. Now he could see what it was, the paint had been scraped off for re-painting. But then the decks and sidewalks neatly swept afterward so the entrance would be clean.

"No. Kayden did all but this side the last few days. I just couldn't stand having her do this hard work, taking care of the bar, the house you're all staying in, and me. Plus, she has Dakota."

"Why don't you hire someone to do this? Neither of you should be doing any of this."

Oakes' lips formed a straight line as he ran a hand through his short gray hair. Pulling the dirty bandana out of his back pocket, he wiped it across his face, head, and neck.

"Can't afford it right now, JT."

JT turned and leaned against the wall next to Oakes. He looked at the paint chips on the ground, all the shapes and colors blending together reminded him of a kaleidoscope. He toed a few of them with his boot, trying to organize his thoughts.

"What's going on, Oakes? Last time we were here this place was hopping. Kayden was off in New York or something, but you were able to pay for a couple full-time bartenders and cooks and waitresses. Now, the place was almost empty when we got here today, and it sounds like you and Kayden are both here at all hours."

Oakes sighed heavily. "We've just run into a bit of a tough patch; that's all." He stood up and walked a few steps to pick up the broom and start sweeping. "It'll get better. We'll paint and spit shine this place back up, and then, once she gets running good again, I'll leave it to Kayden, and I'll retire."

JT watched Oakes sweep. He couldn't help it; he had to ask. "She wants that?"

Oakes looked at him with furrowed brows. "Sure."

JT stood and reached for the broom. "I'll do this; why don't you go shower before Dad gets here. They'll be down soon."

Oakes opened his mouth to protest, but JT ignored him and began sweeping. Oakes slapped him gently on the shoulder and slowly hobbled to the back of the bar to his living quarters.

.

5

J T finished sweeping the paint chips from the side deck of the bar. This place held fond memories for him. Thinking back on it, he thought it weird that he never met Kayden all the times he had come here. She was off staying with someone the first time they came here. The last few times they made the trip out, she was in college, and then she'd gotten a job in New York. Some big fashion outfit or something. Now that he thought about it, Oakes had mentioned his daughter a few times, but JT was just always lost in his own world, dreaming about designing bikes.

He carried the broom to the back and set it against the wall between the two back doors. One door led to the kitchen of the bar, the other to Oakes' living quarters. JT hesitated, not sure if he should knock and make sure Oakes was okay. Rubbing the back of his neck, he rotated his head to ease the tension. This place had fallen on hard times, and still, Oakes wanted to leave it to Kayden? Why saddle her with a bar that would take all of her time running it? No way would he want that.

He turned and faced the garage. Noting the white paint and gray tin roof, it looked to be in decent shape. The two garage doors facing the side road were newer, the windows set in the doors were clean.

There wasn't an outside staircase, which meant it was inside the garage. It would be safer inside, making sure no one wandered from the bar late at night and stumbled upstairs. There were plenty of windows in the upper part of the garage; he imagined the apartment would be bright and cheery. He smiled, remembering Dakota telling him about her pink room.

JT turned and walked around the opposite side of the bar from where Oakes had been working and noticed the wood ready for a fresh coat of paint. He shook his head as the picnic tables came into view with their little flower jars gracing the tops. There were so many unanswered questions here. Opening the door of the bar, the strains of Tennessee Whiskey by Chris Stapleton floated over him along with the cool air from the air conditioning. There she stood behind the bar, thumbs in her back pockets, breasts pushed out. She was watching him. Assessing him. The music system softly crooned the slow, sultry song, and he thought he saw her smile. Damn. His heart began racing, and he honestly couldn't say if anyone else was in the bar because all he could see was her. The first word that came to mind to describe her was 'Angel.' The soft light touching her hair gave the effect of a celestial glow

She had changed her tank top from earlier today. She was now wearing a little burgundy and black lace Harley Davidson t-shirt, which also hugged her body in the most delicious way. As he slowly approached the bar, she cocked her head to the side, and damn, if her eyes didn't get darker.

He pulled up a stool, and she took a step forward, placed both hands on the side rail of the bar and asked, "What can I do for you, JT?"

Her voice slid over him like a t-shirt fresh from the dryer and gooseflesh formed on his arms. He swallowed—he had to—before saying anything. That was a loaded question, and he wasn't sure if he should take the bait and tell her exactly what he wanted – her bent over the bar, ass in the air and him pounding into her until they were both spent—or just order a drink. When he hesitated, she smirked. The little vixen was teasing him.

"You may just get what you're bargaining for talking like that to me, girl." He paused. "If you play your cards right." He looked directly into her eyes and winked, but she didn't flinch. Chuckling, he said, "I'll have a beer. You pick. I'm easy."

She started laughing, a sexy, throaty sound, turned and grabbed a beer from the cooler, opened it, and set it on a coaster in front of him. Smiling brightly, she teased, "I had you pegged for easy this afternoon when I first saw you."

JT smiled, tipped his beer back and let the it slide down his throat. Swallowing, he asked, "That right? How so?"

Kayden shrugged. "You give off that vibe. I've been in the bar business long enough to read people. Love 'em and leave 'em, right?"

"What about you? You love 'em and leave 'em?" he shot back.

She smiled and tucked her thumbs into her front pockets. "You didn't answer me yet."

JT nodded once; she had a point. "I haven't found anyone who interests me enough to keep me around."

"Hmm. What interests you? Have to have the perfect body? Perfect face? Laugh at all your jokes? Worship the earth you walk on?"

JT raised his eyebrows. "Didn't say that. I said interests me. Someone with some substance, a brain, responsible, dependable." He watched her face as he spoke. She had a poker face for sure. "Of course, a perfect body is always appreciated." His face split into a big grin, and she chuckled.

She reached forward and filled a glass with white soda. "I can appreciate a perfect body myself."

The sultry tones of Chris Stapleton's song drifted away, and the stereo system switched to "It's All About That Bass" and they both chuckled.

Oakes walked behind the bar from the kitchen, hair still wet from his shower, but his color had come back to normal, and he looked like he felt a bit better. "Glad you're still here, JT. Let me buy you a beer for sweeping up outside. I appreciate it."

Kayden looked at JT and raised her eyebrows. "You were sweeping outside?"

JT only nodded once, waiting to see what Oakes was willing to share with Kayden.

Oakes interrupted, "How's everything in here? Are we all ready for a crowd for dinner?" He pulled another beer out of the cooler and opened it up. As he set it on the bar in front of JT, he didn't look at him—just turned and busied himself with some notes on the back bar.

Kayden crossed her arms as her father turned his back to her and JT. She stepped back and leaned against the back bar, looking over at her father. "Yep. Are *you* ready?" She watched his face for a long time.

6

The rumble of motorcycles outside signaled the end of the conversation.

A beautiful blonde woman came in, a huge smile on her face and her hair a bit wild. She was laughing and stopped behind JT. Kayden recognized her as Emma, JT's future sister-in-law. She grabbed his shoulders and pulled him around facing her; her brown eyes were bright, and excitement was running through her body.

"JT, you missed it. We saw a mountain lion on the rocks right across from the house. We all took some pictures. Oh my God, you should have seen how awesome it was."

The rest of the group joined Emma in the bar, all talking excitedly about the big cat. JT laughed with his family and looked at the pictures Molly showed him. Kayden wondered what it would be like having a big family. She was an only child, and it was a tough childhood at that. Her mom didn't want children—ever. She ended up pregnant anyway, and Oakes was still in the service, home only periodically. Kayden spent her childhood constantly trying to please a woman who couldn't be pleased. When Oakes came home from the war in Iraq, he was distant, stressed, and tired. Kayden was three or four by that time, and Oakes had all but checked out.

Watching the family before her made her feel wistful. She wanted Dakota to have that—a big happy group of people who loved her. No one would ever love her more than Kayden and Oakes, but she wanted her to know a life better than what Kayden had known. And truthfully, when she watched how comfortable JT was in the midst of his family, she felt a little jealous. He seemed to get along especially well with Emma, which was weird that Kayden felt anything about that, but it irritated her when she watched the two of them talk. She looked over at Gunnar, who was standing next to Emma and seemed relaxed and comfortable.

Oakes looked at Kayden and let out a whistle. She quickly turned and noticed that he was hustling beers for everyone, and she was standing there gawking. She approached Emma and Gunnar. "What can I get you two to drink?"

Emma smiled at Kayden—a genuine smile. "Did you see these pictures, Kayden?" She quickly held the camera over the bar and showed Kayden the proud mountain lion, perched up on the rocks watching below.

"Wow, she's beautiful. You're lucky. We've been hearing about her for a couple of weeks now, but haven't had the opportunity to see her."

As suppertime turned into night, the Rolling Thunder group drank and livened the place up. OK Leathers Saloon hadn't been that full in a very long time, and it was a sight to behold. Kayden had watched them during supper. Oh, who was she kidding; she watched JT during supper and noticed that he was often looking at her. He sat at the end of the table directly facing the bar. She wondered if it was so he could watch her. Whatever the reason, she was glad he did. She rather enjoyed it.

The group stood from the tables and moved over to the bar and Kayden and Jess, their part-time helper, quickly began cleaning up the dishes and tables. Jess hauled the big bus tub back to the kitchen as Kayden wiped the tables down with a wet cloth. She busied herself separating the tables they had pushed together to accommodate the large group and rearranged the chairs. A few more patrons had come in for supper and drinks; a full parking lot will do that. Kayden checked on them to see if there was anything else they needed.

A loud crack signaling the door hitting the wall made her jump, and then the cold dread filled her body; the tiny hairs stood on the back of her neck. The Devils must have seen the full parking lot too and came in to make trouble. Again.

Kayden continued to make sure her guests were taken care of, prolonging the inevitable. Strong arms grabbed her from behind and pulled her into a slightly flabby stomach. The stench of old cigarette smoke and unbrushed teeth assaulted her nose and the arm holding her gave her a little squeeze as the other Devils came in and started yelling. "You all get on out now; this here's our bar, and we don't like strangers and outsiders in here."

A meek couple on the far side of the restaurant stood to go, but Oakes came around the bar and stood in front of them. JT and his family all turned and the men stood. Dog walked over to Oakes, but he kept his eyes on Joci. He pointed to the kitchen and nodded. She gathered the girls, and they all stood close to each other, waiting to see what would happen.

The Devil holding her grabbed Kayden's chin from behind and tried to turn her face toward his, but she resisted. He kissed her on the cheek loudly and then laughed from deep in his gut. Kayden jerked her head and pushed away from him. He let her go easy enough. She rounded on him. "Get the fuck out of here, Boon. You aren't welcome here; we told you that this afternoon. Get!"

She was shaking from head to toe. Her knees would have knocked together if she wasn't so stiff with fear. Her hair prickled and her stomach soured with bile. She couldn't let the stress from these guys throw her right back into the hospital. With the bike rally going on this week, these little visits were happening more often. She suspected that now that Rog was going away, they would continue. Rog was good for something, but that was about it.

The Devils snickered at her. Boon stepped closer to her, but

Oakes moved forward, and Boon stopped. He flicked a look at Oakes, then back to Kayden. She balled her fists and held her ground—her chin out, her back rigid. Kayden swallowed and then found courage. "This is not your bar. These are our customers, and you will not continue to chase people away from here. You hear me? It's ours."

Boon laughed. He looked back and the other Devils, all in torn jeans and black leather vests with a myriad of patches signifying one office or another, all joined in laughing as if Kayden had told the funniest joke ever.

~

JT had had enough of these jerks long before Boon took a step forward. One stride had JT between Boon and Kayden. Lucky for JT they were the same height, Boon was heavier, but JT would bet he was the stronger of them. Boon definitely smelled worse. He straightened his back, pushing his chest out a bit, ground his teeth together, wrinkled his nose and waited to see how this would shake out. Boon stared at him for what felt like ten minutes; the sweat was already forming and trickling down JT's back, and his shoulders were beginning to ache from the tension. The bar was dead silent, even the hum from the beer coolers could be heard.

Boon finally broke the silence. "Aww, look here boys, Kayden's got herself a boyfriend. He's going to defend her honor. Isn't that sweet?" Sarcasm dripped.

Some of the Devils chuckled, but most of them were poised to fight if this went that way. JT continued to stare directly at Boon, his teeth ground together to the point that his jaw ached. He sensed his brothers stepping closer, then his dad stepped alongside JT and directed his comments at Boon. "This bar belongs to the Leathers. It appears you've been making yourself a nuisance. We don't want any trouble, but we're also not going to back away from it."

Boon looked up into Jeremiah's eyes and smirked. "That so?"

The Devils, who had been standing closer to the door, slowly stepped into the bar. The tension in the room was palpable, the heat intense. Jeremiah only nodded once. Boon's eyes shifted from Jeremiah to JT. He floated his gaze over Gunnar and Ryder then Oakes. The remaining Rolling Thunder group who were along closed ranks. Frog and Chase stepped behind the Devils, the other three closing in and completing the circle. JT quickly calculated six Devils and ten of them. They'd be okay.

Boon took a step backward and chuckled. "Well, boys, why don't we leave the Leathers to their guests?"

He took another step backward, and Kayden stepped out from behind JT. That's when JT noticed Kayden had grabbed the back of his shirt. He hadn't felt it before since he was a bit stressed himself, but now, the feel of her hand even knotted up in his shirt felt fabulous. He looked down at her set jaw, the tremble of her lips caught his attention then he saw something in the depths of those hazel eyes that hit him harder than if Boon would have punched him in the stomach—fear. She was afraid, genuinely afraid of these men.

JT turned to Boon, narrowed his eyes and growled. "Get the fuck out of here now!"

Boon smirked. It was sickening the way he looked at Kayden. "We'll be going for now. But, we'll be watching and waiting, and when lover-boy here is gone back to Wisconsin, we'll be back." He let out a sinister laugh, and Kayden shivered slightly, the hand still holding JT's shirt tightened as the Devil's slowly exited the bar. The two Rolling Thunder employees, Chase and Frog, followed them outside to watch and make sure they didn't do anything to any of the vehicles in the parking lot.

JT heard Oakes let out a long breath and slowly walk back behind the bar, his shoulders slightly slumped. Dog and the men followed him and joined the women. Kayden stood frozen for a second longer and then let go. "Sorry. I didn't mean to wrinkle your..."

"Don't worry about it, Kayden. Are you okay?"

JT turned and looked into her eyes. She looked up at him, and he saw the shiny glaze of tears threatening. He reached up and touched her cheek with the backs of his fingers and softly stroked her cheek.

Kayden swallowed and then quickly stepped back, wiping her

hands on the back of her jeans. She softly said, "Um, yeah, I'm good. Let's get something to drink." She quickly walked back to the bar and stepped around behind it. Oakes walked over to her and gave her a hug. JT watched him whisper something in her ear, and she nodded.

7

"Oakes, you need to tell me what's going on here." Dog leaned against the bar, one elbow on the edge. His long hair was pulled into the ponytail he often wore, his build broad and strong; even though you could tell he was in his forties, he held himself well.

Oakes walked to the end of the bar and stood across from Dog, JT, Gunnar, and Ryder. The others were close by, talking softly, the additional customers asking Kayden to check them out so they could leave. Her soft murmurings of apology tightened JT's stomach. Oakes looked over at Kayden and watched her.

"Dakota's father, Rog, is a Devil. He took up with Kayden when she came back from New York. He had worked for me, tending bar and helping out around here for about three months when she first came home."

Sensing her father looking at her, Kayden met his gaze. Her mouth formed a straight line, and she slowly shook her head.

Oakes continued anyway. "Kayden was sick when she came home —weak, and he took advantage of that. He took advantage of both of us." Oakes took a drink from his beer, swept his hand through his short gray hair, and continued.

"We found out about a year ago that the Devils want this land. Rog was initially sent in here to get a job and figure out how to get this place from us. I don't know if he got Kayden pregnant on purpose or if it was an accident. She's asked, plenty of times, but he won't answer." He looked over to see if Kayden was listening. She wasn't, so he continued. "They were willing to let Rog work this all out as long as we didn't sell to anyone else. They had other things to worry about, like coming up with the money. But I think he fell in love with her and couldn't go through with their plans."

"Why?" JT asked. "What's so special about this land?" The thought of Kayden being in love with someone else landed like a stone in his stomach. He could see Rog or anyone falling in love with her; she was stunning. His dick did a workout every time he thought about her. Seeing her made it work a bit harder.

"Mica. It's full of it." Oakes continued. "And, not just mica, but Muscovite Mica. Premium."

Ryder looked at JT and his mouth turned into a frown. "They use that in horizontal drilling don't they?"

JT nodded. "Also in caulks, sealants, powder coatings, and other things." He looked at Oakes. "So this land is valuable—not the bar. That's why they don't care about the customer base. They want you out."

Oakes nodded. "I've owned this bar for twenty-three years, since right after I got out of the Marines. I laid around for a while, depressed and broken, and then a friend told me this place was for sale. I brought Kayden out here to look at it, I guess she was around four years old, a bit younger than Dakota is now." Oakes smiled. He looked over at his daughter and saw her talking to Joci, Emma, and Molly. They were standing at one of the bar top tables and laughing while looking at pictures on their phones.

"She saw the bright red building and the big yard out back and took off running around the place. She squealed, 'Daddy, we have a yard.' That little apartment we were living in downtown didn't have any more room than what we're standing in right now for our whole place. I still remember the look on her face. She lay down on the grass and giggled like I'd never heard her. I bought it right then. For her," he said as he nodded toward the women. "I never knew about the mica until last year, when Kayden started court proceedings to have Rog's custody removed. The Devils dragged us through court over and over, contesting the custody, placement; they ran that girl through the ringer. She was so afraid they'd get their hands on Dakota. Then my attorney was digging up some documents in the courthouse and found some mineral rights papers on this land. Turned out they were included with the deed. Things came together pretty fast then."

JT watched Kayden talking with the women in his life. She looked perfect with them. Like she belonged there. They were giggling and, shit, that smile of hers was stunning. Then she looked over and caught his eye and smiled. At him. It was like a lightning bolt hitting him. The sizzle ran from his head to the tips of his toes. If he didn't know better, he'd think his hair was smoldering.

"You don't have to hang around if you want to get home to your family, JT. The Devils won't come back tonight; they made their point. Besides, they did their duty for today, as you can see," she said looking across the bar, "everyone has left for the night."

Kayden finished refilling the beer cooler, and Oakes came out of the kitchen. "Go on home; it's almost nine o'clock and Payton will be bringing Dakota home soon. I've got this."

He took the empty beer carton from her hands and kissed the top of her head. "Tell Dakota I'll be expecting her for coffee in the morning."

JT's eyebrows raised. "Coffee?"

Oakes chuckled. "I drink coffee; she drinks milk with three teaspoons of sugar and a splash of coffee."

"And you shouldn't be drinking coffee, and she shouldn't be drinking sugar milk. I don't know why you don't listen to me," Kayden chastised.

"Shush. She's the only granddaughter I have, and I want to spoil her and spend time with her." Oakes pointed to the kitchen. "Now go on home." He looked over at JT and asked, "JT, will you see my baby home, please?" Then he bent over the sink and began washing the dirty glasses without waiting for an answer.

"Sure," JT said, but his voice cracked. He'd been sitting here wondering how he'd get her alone. Actually, most of his thoughts were on getting her alone. JT stood, pushed his glass to the edge of the bar and tilted his head toward the kitchen door as he looked at Kayden.

"'Night, Daddy," Kayden said as she kissed his cheek.

8

"You been thinking about getting me alone tonight, JT?" Kayden stopped halfway between the kitchen door of the bar and the garage. She turned and looked up at him, and he swallowed.

"Maybe," he croaked.

"Hmm. Maybe." She turned and kept on walking. He took two long strides to catch up to her. Her hair moved softly in the faint breeze. It was still in the eighties, but that little whisper of wind helped keep the humidity at bay. For the first time, since his first time, JT was nervous. Something about this gal knotted him up. He looked down at her and saw her kick at a stone in the driveway, and he smiled. They reached the door to the garage, and she pulled a key from her front pocket.

She unlocked the door and stepped inside. She turned and looked into his eyes, and he was lost. He reached forward and placed both hands on either side of her jaw, his thumbs caressing her cheeks, his breath coming in short spurts. Her eyes were dark now, almost brown in the faint glow that filtered in from the yard light. She locked onto his eyes with hers and waited. His heart hammered out a swift beat and something he hadn't felt in a long time flitted in his stomach. Much to his surprise, his fingers lightly shook, the anticipation both delicious and unnerving. Unhurriedly he moved closer, giving her time to object. She slowly closed her eyes.

He smiled and then softly pressed his lips to hers. Holding her head in his hands, he moved her head slightly, so their mouths fit perfectly together. Slowly, his tongue teased her lips, then her tongue as she opened for him. A moan escaped his mouth and hers at the same time. Her arms wrapped around his waist and she pulled him tight to her. And she felt...perfect against him. Her lips, soft and pliable, tasted like the sweetest candy. The feel of them moving against his made a shiver slide through him. He wrapped her in his arms tighter and her hard nipples, so damn visible through her tank top, poked into his chest, and his dick grew thick and long. He slid his hand from her waist down to her ass and pulled her into him, and she whimpered.

The sound of a car on gravel caused Kayden to push away from JT and step back. She looked to the ground and swiped at her bottom lip with the pad of her thumb. Clearing her throat, she looked up and softly said, "Dakota's home. I have to get her ready for bed."

JT was dazed. Briefly furrowing his brows, he was about to say something, and then he noticed the headlights of the car approaching. He turned to look and a woman in the front seat waved and smiled as she parked the car. Dakota quickly scrambled out of the backseat and giggled. "Hi, JT. Did you come to see my bedroom?"

He smiled at her infectious exuberance. He wanted to see her momma's bedroom, but he couldn't say that. "Can't tonight, Dakota. Can I take a rain check?"

"It don't rain much here." She looked up into his face and squinted. He kneeled down, so she didn't have to crane her neck.

"Doesn't. It doesn't rain here much." Then he winked.

"Right. Sorry." Dakota looked over at her mom and walked into her waiting arms. Kayden scooped her up and kissed her cheek.

Payton walked toward them, carrying Dakota's pink backpack. "Everything okay?"

Kayden nodded. "JT, this is my friend Payton. Payton, JT. He was just walking me home."

Payton's brows rose into her bangs. Her head slightly cocked to the side. "Pleased to meet you, JT." Payton's bright blue eyes were the first thing people noticed about her. When they looked closer, you could see she was attractive. Her short blonde hair said *no nonsense*; her capris, sandals, and t-shirt said *casual*.

JT reached forward and shook her hand. "Nice meeting you."

Payton smiled and looked at Kayden; she smiled knowingly. "Okay?"

"We had some visitors tonight and JT and Daddy were concerned. It's all good now, though."

Payton glanced briefly at Dakota and then over to JT. She mouthed, "Devils." Kayden nodded. Frowning, Payton said, "Okay. Well, it was nice meeting you, JT. Dakota, darling, I'll see you tomorrow, okay?"

"Bye, Payton. Thank you for taking me swimming."

Kayden set Dakota down and softly said, "Go on up, honey, and start getting your jammies on. I'll be right there."

"Okay. 'Night, JT." She started up the steps as Kayden reached over and flipped a light switch, illuminating the staircase.

JT smiled as he noticed she was wearing a pair of purple shorts and a little purple t-shirt and her red cowboy boots. He whispered to Kayden, "Does she always wear those boots?"

Kayden smiled as she watched Dakota reach the top step and walk into the apartment. "Every day. Daddy bought them for her in Sturgis a few weeks back, and she won't wear anything else, no matter how hot it is outside."

JT chuckled. "Okay. Well, I'll be heading to Sturgis in the morning to set up the show bike at the park. I'll stop by on my way home, though. Will you be here?"

"You asking me on a date?"

JT looked into her eyes and saw the fine crinkles at the corners; then his gaze drifted down to her lips. She was smiling at him and his heart started beating furiously. "You saying yes?"

"You didn't ask."

His voice lowered. "Will you go out with me tomorrow night, Kayden?" He smiled at her and let his fingers brush her jaw, his thumb slightly brushing her bottom lip.

9

K ayden took a deep breath. This man. He was something special. She didn't know how she knew that, but she did. He stood up to the Devils for her, though she didn't know if he knew exactly what he was in for. She should explain that. She owed him that much. Looking into his summer green eyes, she saw a sincerity there that surprised her. But, he'd be leaving to go home in a couple of weeks, so it wouldn't ever be anything serious between them. She'd have some nice memories to keep her company at night when he left. Probably keep her warm at night too, judging by his confidence and the way he carried himself. He admitted that he 'loved them and left them' so he probably had a fair amount of experience.

"Yes, I'll go out with you, JT." She tried to keep her voice from being breathless, but she didn't totally succeed.

He smiled at her and then winked. That wink zinged straight through her, landing between her legs. She resisted the urge to squirm. He reached forward and gently grabbed her chin and kissed her once again. Simple, sweet and too damn brief. "See you around seven tomorrow night."

He turned to leave, and Kayden couldn't help but look at his tight, fine ass. Mighty fine. He stopped and turned, and then the grin spread across his face when he saw where she'd been looking.

"I have a brain, you know," he teased.

She chuckled. "I'm aware. But it comes in a pretty package, and if you don't want the ladies looking, you should cover it up."

"Right now, Angel, I like you looking at it." She tried masking the emotions that just ran through her at the name Angel. It was beautiful, soft, and endearing. No one had ever called her Angel.

He broke into her thoughts. "I was about to ask if you were going to be able to get off work tomorrow night."

She blinked and took a breath to get her head out of the clouds. She was a single mother, bartender, and wannabe entrepreneur. She was clearly no Angel. "Oh." Clearing her throat, she continued, "Yeah. No problem. As you can see, it hasn't been that busy. But it'll start getting busier on Wednesday as all the bikers start rolling in."

"About that. Have the Devils been coming in a lot?" She needed to tell him how awful they were. He needed to watch himself if he saw them.

Dakota opened the apartment door at the top of the steps. "Mama? I'm in my jammies, but I can't find my book."

Kayden looked up at Dakota, then back to JT. "Can we talk about them tomorrow? I need to get Dakota settled and in bed."

JT glanced up at Dakota and waved. Then he touched Kayden's shoulder, and she shivered. "No problem. You'll be okay tonight?"

She whispered, "Yeah. Goodnight, JT."

As he turned to walk away, she quickly added. "You'll watch out for anything...funny on the road, won't you?"

JT tilted his head. "You think they're waiting for me somewhere?"

Her heart began to race. She didn't know, but the thought suddenly entered her mind, and her stomach twisted. "I honestly don't know, JT. They're dangerous and very unpredictable. Just, please be careful."

10

J T stood and wiped the sweat from his forehead with his arm. "Damn, it's hot here," he griped. He was tired and edgy. Since leaving Kayden last night, he hadn't slept more than an hour at a time. Her gorgeous face entered his dreams and didn't leave. He'd dreamed of fucking her sensuous body in every position he knew. Maybe he'd learn some new ones. He'd tugged himself off more than once, and that didn't sit well with him.

Chase, the Rolling Thunder employee with him, had sweat dripping off his forehead. His fine blond hair matted to his head; the minuscule length pulled back into a ponytail of sorts. His arms were covered in tattoos, the skin taut over the muscles beneath. Just the smallest movement was enough to raise the heat level ten degrees, and being inside the trailer was like standing in an oven.

"Sure is," Chase said, turning the wrench on the footboard, making sure it was tight. "All done. Let's get the fuck out of here."

JT straddled his baby—the beauty he'd spent the past three months building. He wanted to win this show so damn bad. *Biker Build-Off* was a sought after award. He hoped that it would also show his father that he was a great bike designer. He knew it wasn't, but it felt like everything was riding on this contest this year. He'd put the pressure on himself; no one else had, but he'd been patient for years. He learned the ropes at Rolling Thunder; he kept his nose to the grindstone; he did everything his father wanted him to do. He knew the business inside and out, and he was good with customers. Damn good. Working with them while designing their bikes would be no problem. It would be a dream.

Slowly backing the bike out of the trailer, a light breeze cooled him down a fraction as soon as he cleared the trailer door. Easing it off the ramp, he stopped and dropped the kickstand. They were behind the building that was hosting *Biker Build-Off*, in a designated area, sectioned off from the other bikes. He stood back and looked at it one more time. Sexy. He'd started with a V-Rod and tore it completely apart. The entire body, frame, and fenders were powder coated pearl white. Chrome pipes, motor and oil tank gave it enough sparkle that she gleamed. The wide fenderless tires created the look of one badass bike. Tough looking, no doubt about it.

A gruff voice yelled out, "Okay, let's go, get 'em inside. Time to get the bikes in and ready for the show." A tattooed bald man wearing a badge with *Judge* written on it walked behind the building yelling as he went, rounding up all the builders. JT's stomach fluttered with excitement. He took in a deep breath; this was it.

Chase said, "Go on, I'll get everything back into the trailer and lock it up."

"Thanks." He began walking the bike into the staging area. The noise level grew, and the temperature was slightly cooler as he entered the building. Large ceiling fans circulated the cool air blown in by the massive air conditioners which were groaning to keep up. The heat outside, the growing temperature inside as it filled with people, motors, and hot metal bikes, gave them a workout. Glancing around to locate his assigned stall, JT tried not to spend too much time looking at the other bikes. He knew the competition would be fierce. Finding his spot, he maneuvered his bike into its appropriate position and let out a long breath.

A large hand clapped his shoulder as Ryder said, "It's perfect, JT. This is it for you. Dad will come around."

JT slapped his brother on the back and nodded. "Thanks. Your support means everything to me. Gunnar's, too."

Ryder nodded. "We've always got your back."

That's when JT allowed himself to look around at the other bikes. He had to wait for the staging judge to come over and check him in before he could leave, but he wanted to see what his competition looked like.

"Have you looked around?" he asked Ryder.

"A little. There are some beautiful machines here, JT. But yours, in my opinion, is top of them all."

JT chuckled; Ryder was loyal, no doubt. "Thanks. Where's everyone else?"

"Having a beer over at Spokes—except my future wife; she's snapping pictures." He raised his arm and pointed across the room. Indeed, Molly was snapping pictures and chatting with some of the builders. As if she knew they were talking about her, she looked up and waved.

The brothers waved back, and Ryder said, "I'll stop back in a bit; I want to go see what she's up to. We can walk around and see what the landscape looks like here."

JT wasn't listening; he was looking through the crowd at a woman who looked like Kayden. Straining to see if it was her when she turned around, he didn't answer. Ryder chuckled and walked toward Molly.

The woman weaved in and out of a couple of the bikes and JT strained to watch her. He hadn't thought to ask if she'd be here. Idiot. Her hair was pulled back in a low ponytail, but it waved and curled down her back, drawing his eyes to the end of it and the top of her sweet, tight ass. Her face turned in his direction and he saw it was Kayden. His cock bobbed in his pants as she reached to the side and slowly pulled a portion of her black tank top from the waistband of her jeans. Two men and a woman standing with her looked at her waist under her shirt and smiled. They continued their conversation as she tucked her tank into her jeans. One of the men wrapped a hand around her waist and then another, gripping her on both sides. Then he stepped back and smiled. JT strained to see what the hell was going on, fighting the urge to yell across the room for the bastard to keep his hands to himself. A small group of people walked in front of him, blocking his view. Once the group moved on, she was gone. He scanned the room unable to locate her.

K ayden stood and looked at her handiwork. Her table was set and she was proud of her display of corsets, waist and leg carriers, full tank garments, and bra tab carriers. This was her first year displaying her handmade concealed carry garments. She'd been working her ass off getting ready for this year's rally. Ever the designer, she had been thinking about this since she graduated from high school. It was why she went to clothing design school. Then she got sick from working night and day, and then Dakota was born. So the idea fell to the back burner of her thoughts. Once she had successfully removed Rog as Dakota's legal parent, she went full steam ahead.

She ran her hand down her stomach to calm the butterflies, but they weren't settling. She wasn't nervous about her garments; those were perfect. No, the butterflies were for JT. She'd looked across the building where the *Biker Build-Off* was held while talking to a high school friend, and there he was. She immediately felt the fluttering in her stomach and the wetness between her legs. He made her feel... different. She was intrigued with him at first, but after tossing and turning all night, she realized this was something else. Every time she remembered how he felt pulled against her body, her face heated, her body responded, and her core dampened. His eyes, the color of new spring grass, looked at her as if he actually saw her. Or was trying to see into her? He'd stood up to the Devils for her, though she had to admit, he didn't know what he was getting into with them. She'd correct that tonight.

"Why didn't you tell me you'd be here today?" His voice was low and sultry, and it floated over her skin like the finest silk shirt. Her body responded quickly, beading her nipples into hard pebbles. She wanted to squeeze her thighs together to stop the throbbing. She turned, and her breath caught. The sight of him up close stole her breath. He smelled slightly musky from the heat, and damn, it made her feel carnal and animalistic.

Looking into those green eyes, her throat dried up before she could respond. Swallowing, she said, "I guess we didn't have time."

"Hmm." He stared at her, never looking away and her hands began to shake. "You always lift your shirt up for men to look at you? Let them touch you?"

Kayden's brows furrowed and then rose high into her forehead. She didn't realize he'd seen her. "Excuse me?"

JT's jaw clenched, and his hand fisted. "I saw you lift your shirt and some man squeezing your waist."

Now she was getting pissed. "What I do and who I do it with is my business." She planted her hands on her hips, and her stance widened as she waited for his response.

JT exhaled slowly, then leaned forward at the same time as he wrapped his hand around her nape. His lips touched hers, softly coaxing at first, then increasing the pressure. More of a demand. He claimed her lips and then her mouth as his tongue plunged in to caress hers. He pulled her tight to his body with his other arm, and she moaned. She fisted his shirt on both sides, and he could feel her shaking. He pulled back just a bit, and she raised up on her toes to recapture his mouth, sucking in his bottom lip and nipping it. He sealed her lips with his and increased the pressure on the back of her head. His dick was hard and throbbing, and he pulled her into him. She felt his rigidity, and he heard her whimper. When they both needed air, he pulled back slightly and looked deep into her eyes.

"I think it's my business, too. Don't tell me you've responded to other men like you just did to me. In public. You kissed me back with the need for more. You were moaning for me, Angel."

"I'm a grown woman, JT, and I..."

"There you are. Hi, Kayden; it's nice to see you here." Molly's voice so sweet and happy broke into the ass chewing Kayden was just about to give him. He smiled as he watched her eyes turn a light hazel as she plastered on a smile for his sister-in-law.

"Hi, Molly. Ryder. Nice to see you today. Have you been looking around?"

"We have. How about you?"

Kayden looked at her table and gestured with her hands. "I'm here selling this year. This is my new concealed carry clothing line. Wanna take a look?"

Molly squealed as Kayden stepped over and began showing off her clothing. JT looked over at Ryder and saw the giant grin on his face. He was staring right at JT. JT shook his head, but Ryder didn't take the hint.

"Gonna get your ass chewed?"

"Not now, Ryder," JT growled.

Ryder chuckled. "I thought you were going to bend her over the table and cut loose. That was pretty steamy, bro."

JT groaned and shook his head. Then Kayden lifted the edge of her shirt again, and Molly reached forward and touched her waist and giggled.

He stepped closer, the snarl on his face growing until he saw what Molly was touching.

JT looked at her waist and saw she had on a dark corset with a gun firmly tucked into the front of it. It was black with a fair amount of lace and bright pink piping dipping into a v and pointing right Where. He. Wanted to be. His penis throbbed and jerked as his mouth dropped open.

Kayden looked over at him, and a smirk played across her sexy full lips. "No waist to see darlin', just a corset."

His eyes slowly traveled up her slim body to her lips. She slowly licked her bottom lip and a large smile played across her face. His eyes continued till he met her eyes. They were crinkled at the corners, revealing a smile on her face. But Molly soon interrupted their private moment as she beckoned Ryder over to look. When Ryder reached out to touch the fabric at Molly's urging, JT thought for the first time in his life that he would punch his brother. Hard. Very hard.

11

Two hours later, Kayden walked into the section of the *Build-Off* building where the bikes were being showcased. The other side was where some of the paid vendors were displaying their wares, which was where Kayden's booth was set up. If she didn't know better, she'd say the universe was conspiring to put her and JT together. Seeing him talking to a couple of guys about his bike, she stood just off to the side. She smiled as she listened to him explain some of the nuances of his bike and the rapt attention the guys were giving to him. As the guys turned to leave, Kayden cleared her throat.

"So, I thought we could eat here in Sturgis tonight, if you don't mind. I know a great stand that sells the best bar-b-que ribs you'll ever taste. They have a small picnic area where we can sit." Kayden moved to stand in front of JT's bike.

He looked up, surprise in his eyes. Then, a slow sexy smile played across his lips and Kayden softly sighed. It was crazy because she wasn't a sigher, but she did it.

"Sounds good to me." JT looked around, then pulled his phone from his pocket and looked at the time. "I can go anytime. It's almost seven o'clock, not many people coming through anymore.

Most of them are out drinking, and they'll be locking up the building soon."

She smiled as she took his hand in hers and pulled him toward the doors leading to the sidewalk and Main Street, Sturgis. They walked quietly for a couple of blocks, weaving around passersby and vendors on the sidewalks. The feel of his work-roughened hand in hers was a thrill. It was strong, firm, and so much larger than hers. She subconsciously squeezed his hand and was surprised that he immediately squeezed back. She turned her head to look up at him. When she met his gaze and saw his heated stare, the electricity shot straight through to her toes.

"It's..." She swallowed and then pointed with her other hand. "It's right here." She stopped and turned toward a little wooden stand at the end of the sidewalk. The bright yellow paint on the outside walls of *The Rib Shack* was welcoming and bright. The red trim around the service window drew your eyes to the server working in the shack. The bright red painted words on the yellow walls, which were clearly hand painted in a hurry, with little droplets of paint dotting the walls, boasted *the best ribs you'll ever eat.* The smoky grilled scent wafted to her nostrils and her stomach rumbled with the recognition that she hadn't eaten in many hours.

"Hi, Dave. How are you?" Kayden said to the man behind the window.

"Hey there, Kayden. People are starting to roll in, and business is picking up. How about you? Been busy today?" His broad smile set into a rugged face surrounded with curly brown hair and reddened lips made him look almost comical.

"Been pretty good." She turned her head and looked at JT. "This is JT. JT, Dave and I went to high school together."

Dave laughed. "I'm actually a bit older; I guess I failed a grade or so." He wiped his hands on a towel and then reached out the window to shake JT's hand. "Nice to meet you. Any friend of Kayd's is a friend of mine."

JT shook his hand and Kayden smiled as she watched her friend and her...what was he? At this point, friend was the best description.

Smoking hot friend who kissed her until her toes curled and her moans escaped without her even knowing it- friend.

"Two racks?" Dave looked expectantly, and Kayden's cheeks tinted pink at the thoughts she was having. "Yes," she said and then stopped. She looked at JT. "Sorry." Her cheeks were now fully reddened. "I didn't mean to order for you."

JT laughed. OMG. The tingles traveling the length of her body raised the gooseflesh on her arms. His sexy full lips stretched into a smile, his white teeth straight and perfect. The crinkles at the corners of his eyes deepened and his face, which mostly was impassive, transformed into a sight to behold. Not to mention the scruff growing on his face that gave him that rugged appearance she found hard to resist.

"Two racks. And, a couple of beers, too." He looked down at Kayden and winked. She didn't drink all that much; she normally had to get up early with Dakota, but a beer with JT would be nice. Especially after he winked at her. Sigh.

Dave nodded his head and pointed with his thumb over his right shoulder. "Go on back and sit down. It's only for special friends, so you should have a bit of peace and quiet back there."

Kayden took JT's hand once again and led him to the back area behind the shack where two picnic tables and a wide array of mismatched lawn chairs sat empty. Taking a seat at one of the picnic tables, Kayden caught JT watching her ass and a half smile formed on her lips. It sure seemed as if he was as attracted to her as she was to him.

"Tell me about your clothing and where this all comes from." JT placed his forearms on the picnic table and reached for her hands with both of his. A tingle ran the length of her body for about the tenth time since meeting him. It was like her blood was magnetized to him. Two opposite poles coming together.

"I've been interested in concealed carry clothes for a long time. Since high school when my dad taught me to shoot a gun. He wanted me to be able to protect myself but what I noticed was there were few options for me to actually carry concealed. Sure, I could put a gun in my purse, but if your purse isn't close by or you need your gun in a hurry, that's a poor option." A helper of Dave's set their beers on the table. She took a drink of her beer to wet her throat. "Holsters offer some options, but they're uncomfortable. And shoulder holsters need a jacket or larger shirt over the top to conceal them. Men have better options. So, I decided I'd design concealed carry clothing for women. They're received well. I've experimented for years on the perfect fabrics and elastics that will hold their shape and color as well as fasteners and then adding style. I like to feel sexy and so do most women, that's why I came up with the corset. It's sexy, durable, and it holds a weapon. The one I'm wearing can hold four weapons. Or, as an option, two weapons, a cell phone and a bit of cash and a clip." The smile spread across her face as she watched JT's expression. Was that admiration?

"That's..." He halted, trying to order his thoughts. "That's amazing. You truly amaze me. When do you find the time with all of the work you have to do with the bar and Dakota and the house?"

She was used to this question. It was usually the first one people asked her. "Dakota goes to bed by eight. I usually work until eleven or midnight. As you can guess, I have a non-existent social schedule."

His voice low and gravely, he said, "I hope that will change while I'm here. I'd very much like to enhance your social schedule." She sighed again. She was turning into a silly school girl with all the tingles and sighing, but for the life of her, she couldn't help it. His beautiful green eyes held hers. She noticed little flecks of brown in them and a deeper green at the perimeter. They were the most interesting eyes she'd ever seen.

"I'd like that."

12

Walking back to their vehicles, Kayden giggled. It was just too much. Three beers after not eating all day, holding JT's hand in hers, the exhilarating environment of Sturgis, life was getting better all the time. She was feeling a bit light headed and frisky.

"I can drive myself back, JT." Kayden stopped at her Jeep and leaned against the front. The streets were less crowded now, but there were still people milling about. She was parked behind the building, and ironically, her vehicle was parked in the same lot as JT's. That crazy universe.

"And, I can drive you back. You can leave your vehicle here and ride back with me in the morning. You've had a few beers; you shouldn't be driving. And, where is Dakota tonight?"

She grabbed the front of his shirt and pulled him close. He leaned in, pinning her to the Jeep. The metal felt warm on her back from the sun's rays, and the scent of JT warmed her in other places. He leaned his head down and nuzzled her neck. Gooseflesh raised on her arms, and a shiver slid through her. She felt him smile as he dipped his tongue gently into her ear then swirled it around the shell. His hand snaked around her waist pulling her closer, right there. She felt him harden as he ground against her and a breath escaped his lips much like a moan. His other hand reached under her hair at her nape and held her close as he kissed her lips gently.

Warm and soft, his lips slid over hers, tasting her mouth fully. He slid his tongue along her bottom lip and then followed it with a kiss before covering her lips with his again. She opened and whimpered as his tongue mated with hers. He tasted like good beer and delicious ribs, and his cologne, heated from his body and the day's activities, enveloped her like a warm blanket. She wrapped her arms around his waist, as much to hang on as to feel him under her hands. The muscles in his back sensuously moved under her fingers as he tensed and pushed himself into her. They were the perfect height for each other; he fit right where she needed him. The thought of people coming by or interrupting them was far from her level of caring. During the rally, Sturgis was a town where anything goes.

JT's hand slid from her waist and easily roamed under her shirt, running his hands along the corset she wore, but he quickly found her breasts and cupped one in his hand. His breathing quickened as he pulled the top of her corset down, allowing her ample breast to fall free. He rolled his thumb over her nipple, forming a perfect peak which he lightly pinched, causing her knees to weaken further. A sigh left her as she gasped and he squeezed it again. Releasing her mouth, he looked into her eyes and she slowly smiled. Her knees threatened to give out, but he held her in place.

"You didn't answer me. Where's Dakota tonight?"

"Payton's," she croaked out. She studied his face in the waning light of day; a small smiled playing on his lips. He pushed his hardening length against her. Right. There. She sucked in a breath and placed both hands on either side of his waist and held him in place as she wiggled against him.

"Damn, girl. You'll have me crazy in about two minutes."

Kayden reached up and cupped her hand on the back of his head, pulling him to her lips once more. Her breathing was ragged, and her skin was heated everywhere he touched her. He pulled back, and she opened her eyes to see his sexy green orbs gazing at her face with a form of wonder in them. Staring at each other for several seconds, she swallowed as a lazy smile drew across his face. Thoughts began racing through her head, making her a bit dizzy, but the main thought was, she had never felt like this before. It was sobering. It was scary as hell. It was also a bit exciting.

"You don't want to do this here, Kayd. I don't want to do this here. I'd prefer to lay you across a bed and slowly taste every inch of you until you need me in you so bad, you'll beg. Then, I'll make you forget any man you've ever been with."

She blinked slowly, her nipples pebbled into firm beads, the ache between her legs almost unbearable. She watched emotions play on his face, his gaze never leaving hers.

"Now, back to driving home. You can leave your Jeep here and ride with me. I'll pick you up in the morning with my bike, and we'll ride in together. You don't need to be driving."

13

Driving along the darkening roads between Sturgis to Shady Pines, his truck hummed as the tires hit the pavement. The soothing sound, the darkening sky, and the soft music made JT feel peaceful. But having Kayden sitting next to him, her perfume filling the cab of the truck teasing his nostrils made him semi-hard most of the ride home. Remembering her taste from not long ago made him lick his lips. Recalling how she felt rubbing against him made him want to tromp the gas and get there sooner. He glanced over at her, sitting with her left foot tucked under her right leg, softly singing to the music on the radio.

"You have a beautiful voice."

Kayden turned her head and looked over at him. Her lips parted in a perfect smile, and he felt the knot form in his stomach.

"Thanks. Daddy says I sing like my grandma, his momma. I never met her, though, so I'll have to take his word for it."

She giggled. And JT had to work hard to concentrate on driving.

"Tell me about Dakota's father. What's the story with him?"

JT saw her reflection in the windshield from the soft lights on the dashboard. She scrunched her face. "He's gone. He worked for Daddy when I came home from school. New York, I mean. I was sick and weak, and he seemed so helpful and interested. One thing led to another, and we sort of got together."

JT bit the inside of his cheek to keep from swearing. Not wanting her to stop, he remained silent, alternating between watching the road and her reflection.

She continued, "Then, I got pregnant, and he floated away. Then Daddy caught him stealing money from the bar right after I had Dakota and fired him. I didn't want to have anything to do with him after that, but he gave me a hard time about Dakota being his and all. I tried to keep it somewhat peaceful because I didn't ever want him taking her for the day on his own. As long as I let him come and see her, things were okay."

She paused and took a deep breath. "By the time Dakota was two, I realized he was deeper into the Devils than I ever knew. I thought he was just friends with some of them; I didn't realize he was one."

JT quickly glanced at her, then back to the road. "Rog is a Devil?"

Kayden nodded her head silently. Then softly she said, "Yeah. He began pressuring me about selling the bar to the Devils. Then he went to jail the first time for theft. He only did six months, but it was enough time for me to put the parental dissolution in place in the courts. He and the Devils dragged things out, made me go to court for every little thing, I almost got sick again from the stress of it all."

She picked at a thread in the seam of her jeans and JT's stomach tightened.

"Sorry. I didn't mean to make you sad."

"You didn't. I'm more embarrassed than anything. I feel stupid for being with Rog in the first place. I didn't love him; he was just nice to me." She looked out the side window. "Pathetic, right?"

"Nothing wrong with liking someone for being nice to you. Sometimes that's how it starts."

"Right. Except, he was only nice to me because they wanted the bar. I was too stupid to see it. Then I got pregnant, but Dakota is the best part of me."

JT smiled as he thought about those cute little red boots, always moving and the pretty little girl years wiser than her age.

"She's pretty special, all right. You're doing a great job with her."

Kayden chuckled. "Thanks. She's a little smarty. Cute as a button and wise for a little girl. She just loves her grandpa."

"What are you going to do about the Devils?"

Kayden shrugged her shoulders. "I don't know." She turned to face him. "I'd be open to selling the bar to them for the right price, but Daddy bought it for me, and he wants me to have it. As long as he's alive, I can't sell it; it'll hurt him."

JT furrowed his brows. He stretched his shoulders forward and then back. A small group of bikes roared past them, and JT watched the tail lights dim as they sped along out of sight. Selling the bar would be the best thing all the way around. Oakes was sick. JT was willing to bet he was sicker than he let on.

"Have you talked to him about it?"

"No, of course not."

"If you don't talk about it, how will you know?"

"Don't say anything to him, JT. I don't want to hurt his feelings. He'll think I'm ungrateful."

JT tapped the turn signal to turn into the lot at OK Leathers. He leaned forward as he saw a man with a noticeable limp scoot from the bar and climb on a bike. When the headlight turned on as he started his bike, the light shined on the broken front door, hanging from the hinges at an awkward angle.

"Look at that," he managed before the man started his bike and peeled out of the parking lot. Another bike, at the edge of the lot started and followed the first one.

"What the hell?" Kayden whispered. Her head immediately turned to look at the front door of the bar. She reached over and unbuckled her seat belt while at the same time unfolding her leg. She had her hand on the handle of the door before JT came to a complete stop.

"Hang on. You can't run in there until you know what you're running into."

"The hell I can't." She jumped from the truck and pulled her gun from her corset before she reached the door. JT slammed the truck into park and jumped out running after her, pulling his gun from his belt at the same time.

14

Stopping suddenly at the open door, Kayden peered into the bar to see if anyone else was around. The lights were on, and she saw some stools laying on the ground and broken glass on the floor. JT stood next to her, and she looked up at him and whispered, "I don't see anyone. You?"

He shook his head and stepped in front of her to enter the bar.

Quietly, he said, "Let me go in first, just in case there's someone hiding." She began to shake her head when he said, a bit sterner, "Please."

Her shoulders lowered as she watched him quietly walk around the door and into the bar, his pistol held up just in case. His steps were soft but the glass crunched under his shoes, and he slowed his gait. Once past the half wall at the entrance, he looked back at Kayden and tilted his head toward the inside.

She slowly followed his footsteps. The odor of beer and gun powder hung in the air. She glanced up at JT, and he nodded but put his fingers to his lips, asking for silence. She nodded once and began scanning the room for anyone hiding. No one knew this bar like she did. There was a storage closet just off the bar to the left as you walked into the kitchen. The kitchen had several nooks and crannies to hide in as well.

But mostly she was worried about her dad. It was still fairly early, and the bar should have been open. Why would someone break the door off its hinges to get in? And where was he? If someone shot off a gun in the bar, he would have heard it from his apartment. Her heart began racing, and she fought off the urge to run in and shout for her dad.

A grunt and a shuffling noise sounded from behind the bar.

"Daddy?" she yelled. JT's brows furrowed and he leveled his gun in the direction of the bar. Kayden followed suit but strode to the open end of the bar.

"Kayd." Huffing out a breath, Oakes was lying on the floor, blood dripping from his head. His pistol laid next to him, glass and spilled beer all around him. "Get. Out." He struggled to speak, his eyes closed, his face contorted in pain. "Not. Safe."

"Daddy, what happened? Who was that?" Kayden quickly dropped to her knees. She reached under the bar for a clean towel and laid it on his head. She grabbed his left hand and placed it over the towel. "Hold this in place and put some pressure on it to stop the bleeding." She looked up at JT. "Can you call an ambulance?"

JT nodded and pulled his phone from his pocket. Kayden watched as he dialed.

Looking at her father, she quietly said, "Daddy, tell me what happened. Was it the Devils? How many of them? Are you shot?"

Oakes groaned as he once again tried to sit up. "No. You need to lie down," Kayden said. "You're cold as ice. I'll run and get a blanket from your apartment."

His voice gravely, Oakes managed to say, "No." He hung on to her arm as he scooted himself to lean his back against the cabinets behind the bar. They both looked up as JT came around and knelt alongside them. Oakes' breathing was raspy and his color pale.

"Oakes, can you tell us anything?" JT lifted the edge of the towel on the top front of Oakes' head. Blood again began pouring out of the cut, and JT put the towel in place and held it there with his hand.

Kayden watched as he took care of her father. He checked his legs for injuries and his chest, abdomen, and back. He reached forward and picked up Oakes' gun and checked the clip. "You shot three bullets, did you hit them? One of them was limping as he ran out."

Weakly, he said, "I got one in the leg. They got the money, though." His eyes welled with tears, and Kayden's stomach twisted. They needed that money so damn bad. But, nothing was worth it if they weren't safe. Now, they were being physically harmed. When would it end? When someone died?

Kayden swallowed her sadness. "It doesn't matter. Were you alone in the bar when they came in? Why did they bust the door down?"

Hearing the faint wail of sirens, Kayden looked into JT's eyes. Her jaw tightened. Her body was as taut as a high wire, her nerves at the breaking point.

He reached forward and cupped her chin. "We'll get the answers we need, but let's get your dad taken care of first. Deal?"

Staring for a few moments, she swallowed then nodded. She'd get her answers. That was for sure.

15

JT sat in a chair in the emergency room waiting area, elbows on his knees, his head bowed down and resting in his hands.

"JT, what the hell happened?" Dog strode toward his son; Ryder and Gunnar close behind.

JT stood and hugged his father and then his brothers as he relayed the story as he knew it. "Dad, there is so much bullshit going on here. I'm worried we don't even know the half of it. The mica might be valuable, but something else has to be going on. The little bit of money that would have been in that till wouldn't be worth committing a crime. It just doesn't make sense."

Dog heaved out a breath, and JT watched his father and brothers take seats alongside and across from him.

Ryder leaned forward. "Where's Kayden and Dakota?"

"Kayden's in with Oakes right now. They stitched him up, but she was needed to answer some health questions. Dakota is with Kayden's friend, Payton, for the night."

Gunnar leaned back in his chair and ran a hand through his short dark hair. His bright blue eyes searched his brother's. "Are you in danger, JT?"

JT's eyebrows raised and he sat back in his chair. His lips turned down into a frown. "I don't think so. Why would I be? They don't know me or who I am."

Gunnar sat forward. "If they're after Oakes and Kayden, you could get in the way." At the furrowing of JT's brows, Gunnar quickly added, "Just thinking out loud, bro, and you should be thinking of all the angles, too. And after last night in the bar, they just might know who you are."

Dog cleared his throat. "Gunnar's right, JT."

JT quickly stood and began to pace. Rubbing his forehead, he turned. "I'm not leaving them by themselves. Clearly, they need help."

Dog stood. "I agree. But we don't know what with. Possibly the Devils. Possibly something more than mica, but we need answers, and we need to be careful."

JT watched Kayden walk toward them from Oakes's room. Her hair was disheveled, her jaw tight, and her back rigid. She looked into JT's eyes. "Daddy's going to be fine. He was hit on the head with a bar stool, and he needed fifteen stitches. His vision was a bit blurry, so they want to keep him overnight. I'll come back and get him in the morning."

JT nodded but continued watching her as she glanced around at his family. Dog stepped forward. "We're here to help, Kayden. All of us. And, I think we all need to talk. Oakes, too." He looked at JT. "We've boarded up the door and locked up the bar and Oakes' apartment."

Kayden let out a deep breath and looked up at Dog. "Thank you all for everything." She turned to JT. "I'm ready to go if you are."

He wrapped his arm around her shoulders and pulled her close. "Yeah. We can go."

He took a step forward and nodded to his dad. "I'm bringing her to the house tonight since we don't know what else might happen there, and she would be alone."

Kayden looked up. "No. I'm not going to the house like some little maiden who needs to be protected. I'll stay at my place."

JT continued pulling her along with his arm firmly wrapped around her shoulders. "We'll talk about it in the truck."

As they walked down the corridor in the hospital, JT heard his father and brothers chuckling behind them.

~

"Do you know what's going on, Kayd?" She swung her head to look at him from her side of the truck. "Did Oakes say anything?"

She pressed her lips together as she slowly shook her head. "He refused to say anything further. Said he was tired." Which is bullshit, she knew he was hiding something.

She turned toward him. "I can stay at my place."

JT had shaken his head before she was finished speaking. "I need to make sure you're okay. If I'm not there with you, I won't know what's going on, which means I won't sleep. Dakota isn't home; there's no reason for you to risk yourself."

"JT..." She stopped at the look on his face.

"Kayden. Please don't argue. It's been a bitch of a day. My nerves have been on a roller coaster with the Build-Off, you, and your father." He blew out a breath, glanced into her eyes and then back to the road. "Let's go hunker down in a big beautiful house, get a good night's sleep and tomorrow we'll get up and assess the damages at the bar, figure out what needs to be done to fix it, and pick up your dad before we head back to Sturgis." He rotated his head. "Already sounds like a full day."

Kayden turned toward the front of the truck and stared out her window. The darkened trees whizzed past her, barely registering what they were. She could see the reflection of the dashboard lights on the glass as her mind wandered to her dad. What was he into? Feeling the truck slow, she turned to look out the windshield as JT turned onto the road to the house. She simply couldn't believe she was spending the night in the big house. She'd dreamed of it, sleeping there, but as the owner and lady of the house, not as a guest. It was bittersweet.

The truck slowed and turned up onto the steep stone driveway; gravel crunched under the tires. The large imposing house nestled halfway up into a hill, stood proudly waiting for her. Light shown from some of the windows, as its occupants had recently returned, probably waiting for them to arrive safely before turning in for the night. Kayden sighed.

JT glanced over. "Don't worry, you've already met everyone. They like you."

She frowned and studied his face in the dim lights from the dashboard. "It's not that," she whispered as she watched his jaw tense.

Her eyes traveled the length of his strong muscular arm, the rippling of muscle, the fine hairs decorating the taut skin. She felt a tingle climb her spine and shivered. His hands tightened on the wheel then released as he reached the shifter with his right hand. He put the truck in park. She watched his nimble fingers turn the keys in the ignition and the motor quieted. Her eyes sought his, and her stomach flipped when they caught and held. His soft full lips hitched up on one side as he watched her assess him.

She heard him take a deep breath, and she stared at his lips. She moistened hers with her tongue, and he growled from deep in his gut. That sexy arm of his reached around the back of her head, pulled her forward and his lips touched hers ever so softly. Light feathery kisses tingled her lips, then his mouth completely covered hers and consumed her. His tongue slipped into her mouth and slid along hers; the velvety softness raised gooseflesh on her arms. His breathing increased and the scent of his cologne made her senses fire with lightning speed.

16

JT pulled his lips from Kayden's and touched his forehead to hers. Willing his breathing to return to normal, he inhaled deeply, and the soft, clean scent of her shampoo and the powdery aroma of her cologne hit him in the gut. Actually lower, but still, like a sucker punch. He lifted his head, the illumination from the house was soft, allowing him to stare into the deep hazel irises staring back at him.

"They're awake and waiting for us. We should go in," he croaked out. She smiled, and his gut tightened. Her full, velvety lips, still damp from his kisses, made him think differently than he'd ever thought. This girl spun his head.

"Yeah," she said softly.

Even the way she said, *yeah* was sexy. She turned to open her door, but he caught her with his hand at the back of her head.

Looking deep into her eyes, he said, "I'll leave you alone tonight, but tomorrow all bets are off." He stared until he heard her sigh and then felt her shiver.

A smirk slid across his lips. He winked at her and said, "Ready?"

She nodded, began to turn toward her door but paused. A sly smile graced her lips, and his heart hammered. Her voice deepened, and the words that floated from her sexy lips stopped him in his tracks. "We'll see if you leave me alone tonight. I'll be sleeping in your bed, naked and lonely."

She slipped from his truck as he stared at the spot she left empty. His eyes tracked her movements, gracefully walking toward the door, her sexy ass swaying slightly, her long hair swishing with her movements. She glanced back at him, and the wanton smile on her face instantly hardened his cock.

"Well, fuck me," he muttered as he opened his truck door and strode to catch up.

Reaching Kayden, he opened the door for her. They stepped into the lower level of the house; the lights above the bar were on, and Ryder, Molly, Gunnar, and Emma were having a drink and chatting. They turned toward JT and Kayden, each smiling.

Gunnar stood behind the bar, leaned down and began pulling beers from the refrigerator underneath. "What'll you have, Kayden?" he asked.

JT placed his hand on the small of her back and led her toward his siblings. When she hesitated, Molly giggled. "Emma and I are drinking Peach Mango Bellinis. Gunnar makes them perfectly. Please join us."

Kayden looked from Molly to Emma then to their drinks. JT reached across the bar and took the beer Gunnar offered him and nodded once. He glanced down at Kayden and raised his eyebrows.

She folded her hands together before her and quietly said, "Sure, I'll give it a try."

Gunnar winked at Emma. "Shall I make another pitcher?"

She giggled and nodded. Gunnar leaned across the bar and kissed her lightly and JT felt a pang in his heart at the love he saw in his brother's eyes. He wasn't jealous of Gunnar in any way, but all of a sudden, he wanted to feel that. He wanted a woman to look at him like Emma looked at Gunnar.

Gunnar slid Kayden's drink across the bar, and JT leaned forward to pick it up. He handed it to Kayden and the room suddenly grew quiet. He tapped the top of his bottle against her glass and downed about half his beer in one drink.

～

Kayden sipped her drink, watching this family tease and share stories. JT was right; it had been an emotional day. As she finished her drink, a tiredness fell over her, and she longed to climb into bed and sleep.

She looked over at JT and saw him watching her with something unspoken in his eyes. Of course, she'd taunted him a while ago; he probably thought she was a cock tease. Twice today she'd laced her commnets with innuendo, and their make-out session in Sturgis still had her tingling deep inside. This family was good. They were just good people, and for not the first time, she wondered if she was getting herself or them into something that would change all of them. They were going home in a couple of weeks. Would she be heart-broken when he left? Suddenly climbing between the sheets with him seemed like a dangerous idea—at least to her heart. Just what she needed on top of everything else, to be shattered and unable to pick up the pieces. Better to steer clear.

Gunnar chuckled at something Emma said. "Okay. I think it's time for my future wife to go to bed." She giggled as he walked around from behind the bar, scooped her up in his arms and started toward the stairs.

"Say goodnight, Emma."

Emma giggled. "Goodnight, everyone."

They disappeared up the stairs as Ryder and Molly stood, and hand in hand walked toward the stairs as well.

"Goodnight, you two." Molly sweetly asked, "Kayden, do you need a t-shirt or something to sleep in?"

Kayden genuinely smiled at her. How sweet. "No, thank you. I'll be fine. Goodnight."

Without thinking, Kayden stepped behind the bar and began cleaning up the dirty glasses and throwing away the empty bottles.

JT came around the bar with her. "You're not here to clean, Kayd."

Rinsing a rag in the sink, she looked up at him. "I can't help it. It's who I am." She swiped the damp rag across the top of the bar, smirking as JT began washing the dirty glasses in the sink. They quietly finished cleaning, each avoiding the next step – the sleeping arrangements.

Kayden stood straight. "I can sleep in one of the recliners out here if you can just get me a blanket from the closet in the bedroom."

"No." His voice broke, and he cleared it as he pulled the band from his hair and rubbed his fingers through it. Kayden watched with rapt attention as his fingers slid through the blond strands, easily gliding along. Her fingers tingled as she wondered what it felt like. The muscles in his arms and shoulders bunched and flexed and she felt moisture gather between her legs and her nipples puckered tightly. He was too handsome for his own good. Hers too.

"I'll sleep out here; just let me brush my teeth and change into sweat pants." He strode toward the bedroom, while she watched his ass, which look fabulous in those tight jeans he wore. He disappeared into the room, and she rolled her eyes in her head and mumbled, "Shit."

17

JT slipped on his sweat pants and a clean t-shirt. It was going to be a miserable night sleeping out there knowing she was in here. He pulled an Army green t-shirt from the drawer and laid it at the foot of the bed for Kayden. He stared longingly at the bed, shook his head, and strode toward the door.

Kayden had curled up in a recliner, her knees pulled up to her belly, her hands tucked under her chin. Her long brown hair fell over her shoulder, the waves cupping her chin. Her thick lashes rested on her cheek. He reached forward and moved the soft silky strands of hair from her beautiful face with his forefinger. She didn't move. He listened to her deep steady breathing and shook his head.

He looked around as if something in the room would tell him what to do, but of course, no answers were written on the wall. He ran his hand across the top of his head and through his hair. Without another thought, he leaned forward and scooped her into his arms.

Her eyes fluttered open, and a soft smile played on her exquisite face, then she closed her eyes again. He strode with her to the bedroom, carefully maneuvering them through the door so as not to bang her head or feet. Gently laying her on the bed, he watched as she rolled over and snuggled into the pillow. Stepping out to the bar area, he checked the door and locked it, turned the light switch off and quietly stepped into the bedroom, closing the door behind him. He leaned down and untied her boots slowly and pulled them from her feet. He grinned as he compared her boots to Dakota's little red cowboy boots. Though she'd look stunning in any footwear she chose, something gave him a little thrill that she wore the clothing that not only reflected her strength but also mirrored his lifestyle.

He thought she'd be more comfortable with her jeans off, but if she woke up, she might think the wrong thing. He did pull her gun from her concealed carry belt, which had exposed itself when she rolled to the side and snuggled into the pillow. Opening the night-stand drawer, he set it inside and silently slid the drawer closed. Remembering the blanket she'd mentioned was in the closet, he pulled it from the shelf and covered her with it. He glanced at the door, but the cold comfort of the easy chair was no match for lying next to Kayden's warmth. Carefully walking to the other side of the bed, he easily slipped in beside her, the king size bed allowing each of them space. He didn't want the space, though, so he snuggled close to her and pulled the edge of the blanket over himself.

She instinctively rolled toward him, and he slipped his arm under her head. He breathed in the scent of her hair and closed his eyes.

Opening her eyes, she saw the soft light that streamed into the room through a slit in the curtains and danced on the bed next to her face. She slowly focused on the room. Registering where she was, she looked at the room through the eyes of an occupant of this house for the first time; normally she was the cleaning lady/caretaker. The deep Scandia Blue color on the walls was her father's favorite color, and she chose this room color for him. She remembered the smile on his face when he'd first walked in here after she'd finished. He told her he was so flattered that she'd picked this room for him. When she'd finished the walls and decorated the room with this comforter in tans and reds, he whistled and stood in the room for a long time, simply looking around at everything she'd done.

She closed her eyes again and exhaled. Her eyes flew open when she realized the slight weight around her waist was an arm. Breathing deeply, the scent of JT floated over her, and her nipples puckered. He always smelled so damn good, spicy and sensual. The man was dangerous to her; she was beginning to feel things for him, and she didn't want Dakota to grow to close to him. That little girl of hers was so loving, and she wanted a daddy so bad. She didn't even realize Rog was her father; he'd seldom spent any amount of time with her, and when he did, it was mostly to watch her play, never to interact with her.

"Mornin'." JT's raspy, sleep-tinged voice, slid over her and kicked her heartbeat up a notch. He nestled his nose into her hair and breathed her in.

He felt good behind her, spooning with her. Then she felt his desire nestled and growing at her backside, and she let out a shaky breath.

She rolled her body, so she stared at the ceiling. She felt the bed dip and glanced up into JT's eyes as he leaned on his elbow over her.

She looked into his eyes. "Morning." She tried not to sound all breathy, but her efforts fell short.

He smiled at her, and damn it all, he was sexy. "Did you sleep well?" His eyes scanned hers, then he glanced down at her breasts, slowly touching her with just a look, then back up to her eyes.

She whispered, "Yeah."

Lust on some men was repulsive, but on JT? Crap, it just made her wet. She tightened her Kegels to make the ache go away, but it made her shiver and feel needy. As he slowly leaned forward to kiss her, she thought about jumping up and leaving the room, but the thought quickly left her mind when his scent swirled around her again, and his hair fell forward and brushed her shoulder, and those damn lips touched hers.

Slowly, his hand slid up her body and caressed her breast, lightly kneading and making her nipples pucker so tight they hurt.

A sigh escaped her traitorous mouth, and he leaned into her, pushing his erection into her thigh. At the feel of his hardness, she arched her hips into his thigh and he deepened his kiss. His hands grew more insistent and quickly he'd moved, so his hand was under her shirt and bra and pinching her tight nipple. It almost made her explode.

Footsteps on the stairs just outside the bedroom door forced both of them to freeze.

"Is he outside?" Molly asked.

A door opened and closed, and Ryder said. "Nope."

"Oh..." Molly giggled.

"Okay, let's go upstairs and leave them alone. I'll talk to him later." Ryder chuckled.

JT exhaled slowly and rolled to his back. He croaked out, "Well, they're up, so we'd better get going." He rubbed his face with his fingers, wiping the sleep from his eyes and rolled to the side, setting his feet on the floor. "What time do we pick up your dad?"

Kayden twisted to her side and rested her head on her hand. "I think around eleven, but I'll call in a little while. I need to go to the bar and see what needs to be done. Then I need to go see Dakota for a while, then pick up Dad before we head back to Sturgis."

She slid to the edge of the bed and climbed from under the blanket. Standing at the edge, she stretched and watched JT lean forward and straighten the comforter and fluff the pillow—essentially making the bed. She cocked her head to the side in wonder. He reached forward and pulled the blanket toward him and began folding it. His eyes met hers. "What?"

"I don't know." She smiled. "I guess I'm surprised you make the bed."

He glanced down at the bed and back to her. "Why?"

She shrugged.

He shook his head and continued folding the blanket, put it back on the shelf in the closet and turned toward her.

"I put your gun in the drawer." He pointed to the nightstand.

She opened the drawer and picked up her gun. Reaching behind her, she slid it into the pocket created just for that purpose in her newest designed belt.

"I'll bet Mom has coffee upstairs; you drink it?"

"Yeah." She glanced around the room and slipped her fingers in her front pockets. She glanced down at her shirt, noting the wrinkles were few; it could have been worse.

As JT walked toward her, she couldn't help but admire the way his t-shirt stretched across his broad muscular chest. His arms filled the short sleeves and extended out in rippled chords and taut skin; the tribal tattoos wrapped their way around his biceps. He looked badass in a wholly sensual way, not like the nasty Devils. He stopped in front of her, and she tilted her head up to look into the green pools of awesomeness she was growing to love. Wait, no. Like, she *liked* his eyes.

"You dealt with a plethora of emotions yesterday, Kayd. I know some of this must feel overwhelming, but I'm here for you and Dakota. My whole family is here for you. Yeah?"

Swallowing the tightness his nearness elicited in her throat, she nodded. "Why?"

His brows furrowed as his eyes assessed hers. "Why?" His voice took on a note of incredulity.

"We barely know each other. Sure, we're attracted to each other." Her hand rose and fell in front of him. "But, you don't really know Dakota or me. We haven't had a lot of time to get to know each other; we're always dealing with shit."

Her shoulders prickled where he placed his hands on them. He dipped down, so they were eye level. "I know all that. Believe me, I do. And, I can't explain it—this feeling." He took a deep breath. "But, it's different; I'm different with you." He stood and raked a hand through his hair, then put his hands on his hips. "It's...just..." He exhaled again. "You're different than anyone I've ever met. For the first time, I want to get to know someo...you."

Her heart raced in her chest, and heat so intense she thought she might catch fire roared up her body. She swallowed to quench her suddenly parched throat, but she couldn't look away from him. And he didn't look away from her—not once. That had never happened to her before, a man looking at her while sharing feelings. A man sharing feelings was new to her—period.

The silence grew between them, and she had no words. She stepped into his body, took his head in her hands and tilted it down to hers and kissed him. Her tongue instantly commanded his mouth, stroking along his tongue; her lips covered his, and her hands shook on his head. She curled her fingers and dug into his silky hair, and a sob escaped her body. Tightening her hold on his hair, she was consumed by him.

He quickly wrapped his arms around her waist and pulled her tight to his body. His hand snaked down to her ass and pulled her into his growing erection, and she whimpered again. He rocked into her, grinding himself against her, hitting her in the perfect spot and she lost control, wrapping a leg around him to hang on.

JT groaned and pulled slightly away from her. She could feel him shaking and knew he was insanely turned on: that made two of them. He lightly cleared his throat and eased back just a bit. "There's a house full of people here." His voice was gruff and his breathing choppy.

Kayden rested her forehead on his chest and felt the rapid beat of his heart, so much like her own. "Yeah," she whispered.

He dipped down again and looked into her eyes. "To be continued." She smiled and nodded. "And finished," he added. He touched her lips with his, then took a step back. "Do you want to use the shower or go up for breakfast?"

She raised her eyebrows; she hadn't thought about breakfast. "Um. I..."

He chuckled. "So, you have a full day ahead and so do I. You're here, and everyone knows it. Take a shower and I can ask the women to lend you clean clothes to wear. You can throw your clothing into the wash while we eat. Once we're clean and fed and talk to my dad about what he and my brothers did at the bar last night, we'll have a game plan for today. And, we'll be ready to face it. Yeah?"

She smiled. "Yeah. If you just get me one of your t-shirts and a pair of shorts or something, I won't need to bother anyone else." She looked around. "Where's my purse?"

He pointed toward the door. "On the bar."

She nodded and turned toward the door. She needed to check her phone and call Payton to explain what happened before anything else. She looked at the clock above the bar—seven o'clock. Payton was surely up with three little ones there.

18

The temporary wooden door creaked and groaned as JT and Gunnar pried it lose from the building.

"How many damn nails did you guys use?" JT griped.

At only nine-thirty in the morning, the sweat dripped from his forehead and trickled down his back—the temperature already a balmy ninety-two.

Gunnar chuckled. "We wanted it secure. Since we didn't know what we were dealing with, we made sure it would take someone a hell of a long time to break in."

The last nail pulled free, and Gunnar grabbed the four-by-eight sheet of plywood they'd found in the garage last night to use for the makeshift door and set it alongside the doorway. Kayden stepped forward, and JT grabbed her hand.

"We'll go in together. Yeah?" He wiped his brow as he waited for her to respond.

Her lips hitched up on one side, and she nodded. "Yeah."

Their feet crunched on broken glass as they slowly made their way inside. It felt creepy as he looked around at the mess. Looking at it in the light of day, he could see how much glass there was. Something he hadn't noticed last night was the blood spatter on the floor.

Bar stools had been strewn about and still laid haphazardly around the bar, and alcohol had been spilled or thrown across the floor. He looked down to see how Kayden was handling it. She swallowed, and her breathing hitched up a bit. He gave her hand a squeeze, and when she turned her gorgeous face up to his, his stomach flipped as his eyes met hers. He turned his head toward the bar and moved them forward. Too much intensity.

JT tried focusing on matters at hand, specifically the men who'd run from the bar last night. Oakes had insisted that it was just some kids needing money, but that didn't make sense, since the bar was barely making ends meet. Any locals would know there wouldn't be much cash. The locals also knew that Oakes had guns and wasn't afraid to use them. His head jerked up; he turned to Kayden.

"How many guns does your dad own?"

Her brows raised into her hairline as she studied his face. "I honestly don't know for sure. If I had to venture a guess, I'd say around fifteen."

"Where does he keep them?"

"A couple of them are in here."

Kayden's steps were loud in the quiet bar as her shoes stuck and released from the sticky mess on the floor. She walked around the bar and pulled keys from her back pocket. Opening a hidden drawer on the side of the back bar, she pulled it out to show a shotgun laid in the cutout and an empty space next to it that only held small pieces of broken glass. He watched her brows furrow.

"He keeps two in here. He always carries in his boot and his back holster. There's a pistol under the bar attached to the underside, in case we need it in a hurry. That's the one he used last night. The police have it now. The rest he keeps in his apartment."

Dog walked forward and looked around the floor behind the bar. Glancing across the bar floor, he turned and caught JT's gaze—his lips forming a straight line.

"So, you're missing one that we know of." He pointed to the empty spot in the drawer.

Kayden lifted the shotgun laying in the drawer from its resting place. She sniffed close to it and looked up.

"This one he bought a few years ago at an estate sale. It hasn't been fired in a while. The missing one is his favorite. A Mossberg 500."

JT watched his father's face and the expressions rolling over it. Glancing at Kayden, he saw a strong but worried woman.

Ryder and Gunnar began picking up the bar stools and righting the tables. Dog scratched the back of his neck and let out a heavy sigh. He turned to Kayden.

"I'll go with you to his apartment and check his other guns. What time is he being released?"

Kayden put the shotgun in its spot, picked up the few pieces of glass laying in the drawer and closed and locked it. She flipped through the keys on her key ring and said, "Around eleven o'clock." She tilted her head toward the kitchen door, glanced at JT, and turned to leave with Dog right behind her.

JT grabbed a broom from the kitchen. Stepping back into the bar, he began sweeping glass, but his thoughts were all over the place.

"Hey. JT?" Ryder spoke softly, his strong arms resting on the bar, his black t-shirt stretched across his shoulders.

"Yeah?"

JT walked closer to Ryder. Gunnar joined them.

Ryder's brows furrowed. "This is weird. What do you think is going on here?"

JT set the broom against the bar and crossed his arms in front of him.

"I don't know. If she knows anything, she's not saying." He pointed his thumb behind him. "There's no clientele here which means no money. We've got a missing gun in a locked drawer. Oakes shot one of those guys last night; Kayden and I saw him limping out to his bike. The blood trail..." He pointed to the blood on the floor. "Leads right outside. Oakes isn't talking. He's saying it's some kids. No way those were kids leaving last night."

Gunnar cleared his throat. "Were they wearing colors?"

JT stared at his brother for a moment. Shaking his head, he said, "I don't know. They parked on the east side of the bar; the yard lights don't shine over there."

He shook his head. "I don't think it's the mica. He could sell this place, but he hasn't. I've asked Kayden about it; she says they don't talk about personal stuff. She won't ask him to sell the bar because he bought it for her when she was little. She doesn't want to hurt his feelings. Same for him."

Ryder shook his head. "That's fucked up."

~

Kayden and Dog walked through Oakes' tiny kitchen and into the living room. The only furnishings were a sofa, a well-worn recliner, two end tables, and a large coffee table with magazines haphazardly strewn across the top. Kayden pointed to a framed photo on the wall above the recliner.

"It's Dad's favorite picture from Iraq." She watched as Dog leaned forward and grinned as he examined the picture. He stood studying it for a long moment; Kayden remained quiet as she let him have his memories. He turned and nodded at her. "We had a good day that day. We'd captured twenty Iraqis and were celebrating on base. Of course, we couldn't have any alcohol there, but we drank soda and talked smack well into the night." He took a deep breath and glanced back at the photograph once more, his finger gently brushing the face of one of the men. "Lance was still alive then. He was killed two weeks after this picture was taken."

Kayden cocked her head. "Lance?"

Dog's voice hitched, "My best friend."

Nodding, she suddenly remembered her dad telling her about Lance saving Dog's life and losing his own in the process.

Quietly, she said, "I'm sorry for your loss."

Dog nodded once and heaved out a deep breath. Looking toward the coffee table, he held out his hand. "Shall we?"

Kayden knelt in front of the table, inserted a key into a lock just under the top and slid open a secret door revealing four perfectly placed pistols and two more shotguns. Both of them looked into the drawer and saw each spot filled. Dog leaned back and looked around the room. "Any other hiding spots?"

Kayden stood and wiped her hands on her jeans. "Yeah, in his bedroom."

She led the way into the bedroom, and the first thing she noticed was that the bed was unmade, and the room smelled stale from being closed up. Her father was usually meticulous. There was some other unusual odor; she couldn't place it. Wrinkling her nose, she knelt in front of the nightstand and unlocked the door. She pulled out the upper hidden drawer and there lay two more pistols. She looked up at Dog. "I don't know of any other hiding places." Looking into the bottom of the nightstand, she saw a metal box laying on the bottom. She pulled it forward and flipped the top. Her eyes were transfixed by the pile of cash laying in the bottom. Hundreds, fifties, and twenties—no small bills. She quickly closed the lid and latched it. She shoved it to the back of the nightstand where it had been. Her heart hammered in her chest after seeing the stash of cash. She'd wondered here and there about how her dad had money when things were tight. He always said it was from his savings, but people don't usually keep their savings in a lockbox in their house.

She wanted to talk to JT about it and get his thoughts; she knew he was suspicious of the situation and the growing dread in her stomach that her father was involved in something illegal was beginning to burn. As soon as that thought flitted through her head, her fingers shook, and her head began to pound. JT would be leaving soon. She'd need to deal with all of this herself.

Dog stood—big and imposing—watching her eyes. Fighting the urge to cry and scream, she quickly ushered Dog from the room.

"We should go." She quickly brushed past him and into the living room.

"What's going on, Kayden?" His jaw tightened. "If Oakes is in some trouble, I'll try and help him."

She walked through the living room to the door. "I've got to go and see Dakota," she said as she opened the back door.

They stepped outside and his cell phone rang. He glanced at the screen and said, "It's the shop; I'll be a while here." She took that opportunity to call her high school friend Chris, their local contractor extraordinaire to come and fix the door and their helper, Jessie, to come in early and clean the bar. She waved to Dog and walked into the bar through the kitchen door.

She stepped into the bar, still holding her cell phone. She needed to put some space between herself and the Sheppards. She was starting to rely on them too much, and there was something her father wasn't telling her that she needed to figure out.

She walked up to JT, her spine stiff and unyielding, her neck tight. She rotated her head and heaved out a breath.

"I'm going to visit with Dakota for a while. I need to explain that Grandpa had an accident and talk to Payton about some things. I have Chris, a friend, coming to put a new door on, and Jessie, our part-time worker, is coming in to clean. I'll see you around, 'kay?"

She turned to leave before he could say anything and bolted from the bar into the kitchen. Her hopes that he'd just leave her alone were dashed when he caught up to her.

He raised his voice and grabbed her arm, spinning her around. "What the hell is going on now? You come back from your dad's apartment, and suddenly you're bolting out the door? And who is Chris? And, how are you going to pick up your dad?" He scrubbed his hand down his face. "What the fuck is going on, Kayden?"

She watched the hurt in his eyes and swallowed. She had to get away from him; she was starting to feel things she had no business feeling.

She kept her voice low and even. "I don't need to explain myself to you, JT. What I do is my business. Where I go is my business." She turned toward the back door, unable to look at the pain and confusion in his eyes.

Taking long strides to the garage, she unlocked the service door and quickly closed it behind her, immediately turning the lock. She strode to her bike and straddled the seat. She took a few deep breaths to calm herself and reached forward to turn the ignition switch on. She hit the garage door opener and took a deep breath, bracing herself in case JT followed her.

She was relieved and a little disappointed to see he wasn't standing there. She eased her bike out the door, pushed the button on the control in the bag on her windshield and glanced around. Dog was still standing alongside the building talking on the phone. He waved to her, and she let out a long breath and nodded.

Turning off her road onto Main Street, she breathed in deep as the wind whipped her hair and floated over her body. The heat diminished on her bike—everything did, including her worries.

She navigated past the general store and the little liquor store. She waved at her high school friend, Stacey, and her kids, as they walked toward their car parked on the street. She slowed at the stop-light in front of the hardware store where her friend Chris was just leaving carrying her new door. She pulled in next to him, and sat on her bike as he loaded the door in the back of his truck. He came back around his truck and swept his fingers through his curly brown hair.

"What's up, Kayd?" His voice was a deep rich baritone. She'd told him all through high school that he should be in radio. He'd just shake his head and tell her he wanted to build things. He'd helped her with the bar here and there, and she was grateful he did it for drinks. Having friends was a good thing.

"Same old shit, Chris. Thanks for taking care of this." She smiled at him, and he nodded.

"I'm on my way to the bar right now. Sorry this happened. Know who it was yet?"

She frowned and shook her head. "No. Dad says some kids, but I saw them get on Harleys and take off. Not kids. I just don't know anything these days. The police are looking into it."

She shook her head. Chris patted her shoulder.

"It'll get better, Kayd. Drive safe on that thing, and for God's sake, put a helmet on, would you?"

Kayden saluted and walked her bike backward from its parking space. "I'll be fine. Dad's friends from Wisconsin are at the bar right now. Treat them right, okay?"

Chris cocked his head, his brown eyes questioning. "You left them there?"

She nodded. "I needed to get away. Gotta go see Dakota."

Turning the ignition switch on, she pushed the starter button. Her bike roared to life, and she checked for traffic before pulling out onto the road.

19

JT stood in the kitchen and watched out the door as Kayden took off on her motorcycle. Damn woman was infuriating. Too independent for her own good, and damn it all, she looked sexy as hell on that bike.

He heard his dad talking and turned his head in that direction. Seeing his dad walking toward the door, cell phone to his ear, he pushed it open to let his dad step in. Tucking his phone into his pocket, Dog nodded at JT.

"What the hell happened to make her run off like her tail was on fire?" JT blasted his dad.

Dog looked at him, his brows raised and shook his head.

"She found the guns locked up in the gun cabinet and nightstand, and a metal box in the bottom of the nightstand. She opened it up, and I couldn't see for sure, but it looked like a large amount of cash in the box. She bolted up and ushered me out as quickly as she could."

Dog let out a long breath. "I'm going to see Oakes and find out what that old man has gotten himself into. You guys good here?"

Watching his father's eyes and the stern set of his jaw, JT saw worry. "What does your gut tell you, Dad?"

Pulling a bandana from his back pocket, Dog tied it around his blond head, securing it in the back. "I'm afraid to venture a guess, but he's been my friend for a long time, and I want to help him."

JT followed his father walking from the kitchen to the bar where his dad addressed his brothers. "Boys, I'm heading to the hospital to see Oakes. I've called your mom and let her know. When I get back, be ready to head to Sturgis; we should be there no later than noon."

Catching glances with each of his brothers, he tightened his jaw. He shrugged his shoulders and looked at the time on his phone. Nine forty-five. Already so much bullshit for this early in the day. This trip sure as hell wasn't turning out as he'd planned. Hell, he'd barely given ten minutes of thought to the Build-Off today. It'd been all he thought of two weeks ago; now all he thought about was Kayden and helping her and Oakes.

The door opened and a tall curly headed man walked in. About to tell him the bar wasn't open, the man held his hand up in a wave and said. "I'm Chris. Kayden asked me to come and replace the door. I take it you're her Wisconsin guests?"

"Not sure I would call us guests. Not sure what we are." JT stepped forward and shook Chris' hand. "I'm JT. These are my brothers, Ryder and Gunnar." He waved his hand toward his brothers who both stepped forward to shake hands with Chris.

Sizing Chris up, he asked, "How do you know Kayden?"

Chris chuckled. "I went to high school with her."

JT's jaw ticked as he clenched his teeth. His back was rigid.

Chris stared at him for a long while then a grin spread across his face. "She's smart, Kayden is. She's independent; she's had to be. She's also infuriating and a bit of a free spirit."

Letting out a long breath, JT said, "Yeah."

Gunnar and Ryder chuckled behind him as they continued fixing a table. Chris' gaze traveled to them and back to JT. His voice lowered. "She's worth it, though, if you can tie her down."

JT shook his head. "Nobody's tying anyone down."

A grin spread across Chris' face. He nodded once and turned

toward the opening he'd just walked in. "I'll be putting the new door on if you need anything." He glanced at Ryder and Gunnar and waved his hand as he strode out the door.

20

Kayden pulled into Payton's driveway and turned the ignition on her bike. Dakota came running out the front door. "Mommy! I'm so happy to see you."

She stood from her bike and kneeled down to scoop her beautiful little girl into her arms. She hugged Dakota close, and little arms squeezed around her neck and small lips planted noisy kisses on her cheeks. This was a healing balm that no one could bottle and sell.

"I missed you, Kota. Were you a good girl for Payton and Duncan?"

Dakota giggled, and Kayden closed her eyes. That was the best sound in the world. "Duncan came home late last night. There was some drugger in the park."

Setting Dakota on her feet, she sighed. "What's a drugger?"

Dakota's tiny head tilted up to look at her. "You know—a bad guy."

Glancing toward the front door, Payton stepped out onto the sidewalk cute as ever. Her sassy hair cropped in a short style always looked perfect. Her long thin legs bare from the bottom of her denim shorts down were model perfect. Suddenly a pang of insecurity hit Kayden in the gut.

Payton leaned into her and hugged her tight. She whispered in her ear, "You're wearing the same clothes you had on yesterday."

Pulling back, she stared at her friend, a sly smile on Payton's face. "We have a little bit to talk about. And, I could use some more coffee. Not nearly enough today."

"Come on in. I've got a fresh pot for us to sip on." Payton looked down at Dakota. "You want to let Mommy and me have a cup of coffee while you, Catcher, and Ruby finish your cereal?"

Dakota squealed. "Momma. Payton's letting us eat our cereal in the living room and watch cartoons. At the same time."

It was hard not to laugh, Dakota's excitement was so real. "You're one lucky girl."

"Yeah. Ruby's lucky, and Catcher is, too."

"Yep. Go on in; we're right behind you." Kayden looked at Payton. "You're spoiling her."

Payton laughed. "It's more for me, really. Duncan got home late last night, and we sat and talked afterward. So, I'm moving slow this morning. Let's go talk about why you're still wearing yesterday's clothes and what's going on."

Kayden sat at the kitchen table, her fingers wrapped around her coffee cup. She'd finished relating yesterday's events and waited for Payton's words of wisdom.

"Well. I think you two need to get horizontal without clothes and see where it takes you. He's smoking hot; I'm surprised you haven't jumped his bones yet."

Kayden chuckled. "There's something different about him. It...he scares me in a way."

"Hmm. Maybe because he's special?" A teasing smile formed on her lips.

Shaking her head, Kayden took a sip from her coffee and pondered what special meant. "I can't let myself think like that. And, I can't let Dakota think like that either."

"Why on earth not? You've been put through your paces with Rog, and before that, your nervous breakdown. From what you've told me, this guy seems like the genuine deal. I think it's stupid to let him walk

away without ever knowing if you two could be good together."
Payton stood and brought the coffee pot over, refilled their cups, and
placed it back in the maker. "At least have some hot monkey sex first,
for crying out loud. There's no one around here that looks like him."
She fanned herself for effect.

Dakota skipped into the kitchen and climbed into Kayden's lap.
Kissing the soft hair on the top of her head, she closed her eyes and
held her daughter close. Dakota turned around and looked into
Kayden's eyes. "Is Grandpa mad that we didn't have coffee this
morning?"

Kayden glanced at Payton quickly, then looked into Dakota's
earnest eyes and said, "Grandpa had an accident last night. He
bumped his head, and the doctors wanted him to spend the night at
the hospital so they could make sure he was okay." Smoothing Dakota's cheeks with her fingers, she continued. "He's fine, and I'm going
to pick him up in a little while. Would you like to come with me and
then I'll bring you back here before I head back to Sturgis?"

Dakota nodded. "I wanna go see Grandpa." Tears formed in her
eyes and Kayden quickly hugged her close.

"He's just fine baby girl, but you come with me, and you'll see for
yourself. Okay?"

Dakota nodded her blonde head and swiped at her eyes.

Setting her down, she said, "Go get yourself dressed, and
we'll go."

Watching her sweet daughter with a heart of gold walk from the
kitchen, the lag in her step weighed heavy on Kayden.

Turning to Payton, she asked, "Can I borrow your car for a little
while?"

"Of course, you can."

Nodding, Kayden reached across the table and took Payton's
hand. "Thank you. Now tell me, what's going on at the park?"

Payton squeezed her hand. "I thought Duncan being a park
ranger would be a safe, comfortable job, but last night they ran across
a growing operation right in the park. That's a federal offense. It's big,
Duncan said. Now I'm worried he might be in danger. Whoever has

balls big enough to grow marijuana in a state park certainly isn't going to be too happy with the rangers who will be destroying their crop."

"Shit. That's bad. What on earth is going on in this town? The Devils, robberies, now pot growing operations? Lord, Payton, this is bad."

"My thoughts exactly."

21

Kayden walked into Oakes' hospital room holding Dakota's hand. Dog was sitting in a chair facing Oakes as he sat on the side of his bed, fully dressed in the jogging suit Dog had brought him. He looked tired and weary.

Dakota ran to her grandfather and he helped her climb up onto the bed. She looked at his bandage and then into his eyes.

"Are you better now? When Mommy puts a bandage on my owies, I feel better."

Oakes chuckled and nodded. "I'm good, Kota. Did you have fun last night at Payton's?"

"I had fun. I'm sorry we didn't get to have coffee today. I'll be staying with Payton a bit while mommy sells her conceal clothes at Sturgis."

Oakes hugged her tight and looked over her head at Kayden.

"I know, little one, but we'll see each other every day. Okay?"

Kayden walked over to him and kissed the top of his head, alongside the bandage that covered a good portion of it.

"They shaved some of my hair last night. Gonna be hard attracting the ladies with half my damn head shaved." His voice was gravelly and weaker than usual.

Kayden and Dog chuckled. She stood back. "Seems the last thing you should be worried about is the ladies." Looking at Dakota and back to her father she continued, "Language."

Oakes looked up into her eyes, nodded his head once.

"We've been at the bar this morning, cleaned most of it up. Jessie's there right now cleaning the floors. Chris is putting a new door on the building."

She glanced at Dog then to her father.

"Your Mossberg is missing." Her voice was tight, her lips thinned.

She watched her father's eyes droop and he lightly shook his head. His refusal to look at her made her suspicious.

Her voice rose. "You knew that last night and you didn't say anything?"

His sad eyes looked into hers. "I didn't want to worry you. JT was there to take care of you and I hoped you'd get a good night's sleep and we'd deal with it all today."

Kayden glanced at Dakota and then to her father. She looked at Dog. "You get anything out of him?"

Dog shook his head. Kayden's lips turned down, her brows furrowed.

"Mommy, you're not supposed to do that with your eyebrows; you get lines. Remember?"

Kayden chuckled. That girl remembered everything. "Sorry. You're right and I'm glad you reminded me."

Dog stood. "I'll take off." He turned to Kayden. "We're leaving for Sturgis at eleven o'clock. We'll pick you up at the bar."

"I can just…"

Setting his jaw, he sternly said, "Be ready and stop running." He turned to Oakes, walked the two steps forward and shook his hand.

"I'm here. I'm available and I want to help you." He patted Dakota's head, looked into Oakes' eyes and said, "Being stubborn might only make things worse." He glanced back down at Dakota.

Turning, he said to Kayden, "See you at eleven." Then strode from the room.

Kayden huffed out a breath and plopped into the chair Dog had just vacated. Her eyes met her fathers. "What?"

"What are you running from?"

Kayden's lips formed a straight line. "Nothing."

She picked at invisible lint on her jeans. Oakes cleared his throat. "JT?"

Dakota looked up at her grandfather. "I like him, he's nice."

Oakes shook his head. "I agree, so is his daddy and his whole family." He looked into Kayden's eyes. "You could do so much worse."

Abruptly standing, she released a breath. "Are you ready to go home?"

22

Kayden pulled her motorcycle into her garage. She was already weary from the morning she'd had and there was a full day ahead of her. Climbing the stairs to her apartment, she glanced down to look at her bike and the empty space where her Jeep usually sat. The garage was hot, though the shade from the sweltering sun gave her some relief.

Today she needed to focus and make connections. Finding people who loved her clothing and accessories was vital to get her a jumpstart on being self-sufficient. It was beginning to be clearer she was going to need to be, and the bar was a thing of the past. Eventually, she'd need to talk to her dad about selling it and moving on. If the Devils wanted it that bad, they could have it, but it stuck in her craw to have to let them have their way. Bastards.

She stepped into her kitchen and took a deep breath. The fresh clean scent of the air freshener plug-in washed over her along with the cool blast from the air conditioner. It felt like she'd been gone from here for weeks. She laid her keys on the wooden table against the sage green wall and glanced at the cute little floral arrangement Payton had made for her when she first moved into the garage three years ago. She took a glass from the cupboard and filled it with water from a pitcher she kept in the fridge. Leaning against the counter, she drank her water and glanced at the clock above the stove. She had half an hour to get ready, then she had to face JT. He was more than likely pissed, maybe hurt. She hoped he wasn't the type of man who screamed and yelled when he was pissed. She'd had enough of that with Rog. He was always pissed.

She showered, shaved her legs, blew her hair dry. The natural curl worked well for her sometimes, though she tried to straighten it often. Today she piled it up in a messy bun and let the waves flow around her head. She donned an Army green sleeveless blouse with a sweetheart neckline and blingy buttons down the front. A short, denim skirt and her brown cowboy boots finished off her outfit. Adding a bit of makeup to give her a smoky eye and gloss to her lips, she admired herself in the mirror and realized she wanted JT to think she was beautiful. Damn it all if she didn't think he was something short of perfect and a damn fine man. Payton was right, if she didn't give them a try, she'd never know and always wonder. That was, if he was still interested.

Hearing motorcycles pull into the bar parking lot, she glanced out the window facing the road. The Rolling Thunder group was there and she needed to get a move on. She grabbed her purse and keys from the table and opened the door to her apartment. As she began descending the stairs to the garage, her heart stopped when the service door opened and JT stepped through it and then locked the door. His posture was rigid, his jaw clenched, his gorgeous mane of hair pulled back into a ponytail at his nape, a black Rolling Thunder bandana wrapped around his head. The black t-shirt he wore stretched over his broad shoulders while the fit of his jeans formed the most delicious ideas in her mind. He simply exuded a sex appeal that was impossible to resist, even if it broke her in the end.

She stepped off the stairs and walked two steps toward him, holding his gaze with hers. "Hi," she whispered.

He nodded.

Okay, mad was definitely front and center.

"I owe you an apology for running this morning. I'm very sorry," she whispered.

His jaw tightened again but he never looked away from her. Her heart hammered in her chest; his scent and the muskiness of just him in the heat swirled around her and made her light headed. She lay her palm gently on his chest, stood on her toes and lightly touched her mouth to his. At first he resisted, not opening his mouth to her. She pushed her breasts into his chest and wrapped her arms around his waist. She pulled her lips from his, just a fraction, and whispered, "Kiss me, JT."

He hesitated only for a moment before his hands shot out and pulled her hips into his. His kiss was searing and the hunger with which he devoured her lips made shivers run the length of her body and settle between her legs. He reached down and pulled her skirt up, quickly grabbing her ass and she hitched her leg up and wrapped it around his legs as she whimpered.

He walked her back deeper into the garage, until they were next to her bike. His voice gruff, he asked, "You want this now?"

"Yesss," she hissed.

He quickly spun her around and gently pushed her shoulders forward, so her hands lay on the back fender of her bike. She felt her panties pull down her legs, then he lifted her leg and pulled them off of one leg and let them lay on the ground. She kicked them aside and heard his zipper and clothing rustle and a package crinkle, then she felt his hands rubbing her ass. His breath next to her ear, he nuzzled her neck and breathed in the scent of her hair.

Gruffly, he said, "This morning when you sped out of here on this bike, I was pissed. But, you're sexy as hell on it and my thoughts quickly turned to having you, like this, as soon as possible." His hands continued to massage her ass, the work-roughened pads such a contrast to her soft skin, then his fingers slipped inside her wetness, and she hissed as his fingers slowly slipped in and pulled out. "Seems like you like this, Kayden."

She dropped her head between her arms and closed her eyes. It'd been so long since she'd been touched, it felt like heaven. Her eyes moistened and her knees quaked. Then she felt a sharp slap on her ass and she yelped. Her head shot up and she began to stand, but he held her in place with a hand on her shoulder. His head close to her ear, he whispered, "That's for taking off like you did without any explanation."

His calloused hands rubbed the spot he'd just slapped, soothing the sting. Another slap on the other cheek had her hissing out a breath. "That's for not trusting me to help you when I've shown you over and over that I'm here for you."

He gently massaged the sting and she whimpered. That was unbelievably hot and she was so turned on she thought she'd scream at any moment. Feeling his hands on either side of her hips, she felt the tip of his cock at her opening but he stood still.

"Tell me when you're ready," he groaned.

It didn't take her a second before she begged. "Yes. Now. Please."

He chuckled and then very slowly slid inside of her. Her release of breath in the steamy garage sounded unbelievably loud. Her elbows shook from the excitement, her knees still quivered. He urged her feet wider apart, opening her up to him. She was completely vulnerable and open and had never been more excited in her life.

His pace increased, his length filling her completely before pulling out and leaving her empty and wanton. As he slid back in, she heard him groan and increase the pressure on her hips with his fingers. Their thighs slapped together, the pace became fast and furious. She felt her skin grow dewy, she could feel the blood rushing through places it hadn't been felt in years. Three years, to be exact.

"Are you ready, Kayd?" he gruffed out and pushed in hard two more times.

She managed to hiss out, "Yes."

He leaned forward and ran his fingers in circles over her clit and she moaned loudly. She heard him growl and increase the motion as he moved in and out of her. His ragged breathing in her ear was the end of her, and she tumbled over the edge, crying out as her orgasm sped through her. He thrust a few more times until he groaned loudly. She could feel his heart beat against her back and his cock pulsing inside of her. Sexy.

Slowly, he pulled out of her and she lowered herself to her elbows until she could stop shaking. He wrapped an arm around her waist and pulled her up to stand, she turned to face him. His smoldering gaze held her attention for long moments. He pinched the end of the condom and pulled it off, hitched up his pants and walked to the corner, dropped the condom in the wastebasket, tucked himself into his jeans and zipped up. He walked to her and kissed her lips. "You drive me crazy, Kayden."

One side of her lips hitched up. "You drive me crazy, too, JT."

She looked down at her blouse, straightened the hem then cocked her head toward the stairs. "We can go and clean up before we have to go face everyone at the bar."

He simply nodded.

23

Following her upstairs was difficult because all he could think about was that her panties were in her hand and her ass was right in front of his face. But they had a bar full of people waiting on them, so time was running short. The cool air hit him first as the door opened, but then the clean scent of her apartment soothed him where he'd so recently been irritated and then aroused by her. The apartment smelled like her and it felt like a balm on a wound.

She turned her head and looked into his eyes. "You can use the bathroom first; it's this way." Her smoky voice elicited shivers of excitement in him. They continued down the hallway and she reached into a darkened room and flipped a switch, illuminating a tan bathroom with a wicker framed mirror over the sink. She stepped aside and a sly smile spread her lips. "I'll go slip on a clean pair of panties." She pecked his lips and glided into a room just down from the bathroom. Oh, what he wouldn't give to follow her in there and have the whole afternoon to play with her any way he'd like.

After cleaning up and forcing himself to turn toward the living room, he looked out the window over her sofa and saw a smaller shed behind this garage. It had an extra tall garage door on it and a service door alongside. It butted up to the hill behind it, giving the impression that it was built in it, which seemed rather strange, but so did a lot of things.

The air changed in the room, and her presence was felt, creating gooseflesh on his arms.

"What are you looking at?"

"How long has that shed been here? I don't remember it." He turned to look at her and his eyes locked on her shiny lips.

She shrugged a shoulder. "A few years. Dad built it to store his motor home. He bought it after mom died, which was..." She bit her bottom lip and cocked her head. She was adorable. Her eyes looked sexy today. She had different makeup on and he wondered...no, he hoped it was for him. "I guess it's been about fifteen years ago now. We were going to travel the country in it as soon as I graduated, but I guess as I got older, he realized I wasn't going to be around to do that since I wanted to go to New York. But, he kept the motor home and said it'd be a good way to retire."

JT watched her glance out the window, a little frown marring her lips. "Of course, who knew I'd be home so soon and sick on top of it?"

She shrugged and looked into his eyes. HIs brows furrowed and his head cocked just a fraction. "Not sure if Dad told you, I had a partial nervous breakdown. New York life just wasn't for me, I guess."

He swallowed. "I'm glad you came home. I'd never have met you otherwise."

Her brows rose into her hair and she tilted her head to the side slightly, an action he was growing to love. It made her seem vulnerable and shy. "That's really nice to say. I'm glad I met you, too."

The honking of a horn broke the spell that was spinning around them. He glanced toward the door and then back to her. "We're driving the chaser truck today, so we need to go. You ready?"

She nodded and stepped into the kitchen and grabbed her purse from the table. He opened the door for her and nodded as she moved onto the landing. He turned the lock before stepping out. They went down into the garage and he couldn't help himself; he had to look over at her motorcycle. That was a memory he would relive over and over the rest of his life. He'd never spanked a woman before, and he had to admit he enjoyed it. The look of her smooth round ass tinted pink where he smacked her, her muscles bunching afterward and her moans, was dream worthy.

They walked out of the garage and toward the bar together, entering through the kitchen door. The first face he saw was Ryder's as he entered the bar and the grin on his brother's face made his flame a bright red. Gunnar chuckled and his eyes shot to his brother's in a flash. Soon every one of them was looking their way, and the room seemed far too silent to have all of these people in it.

Oakes was the first to say anything. "What took so damn long?"

Kayden's face burned bright red and she looked at the floor for a split second before squaring off with her father. "Don't see what difference it makes how long it takes me to get ready. Since I've been running to the hospital and back, I haven't had a minute to myself."

It was Oakes' turn to be embarrassed. He rubbed his fingers over the bandage on his head and flicked his eyes to JT, then back to Kayden. "Sorry, Kayd."

The silence stretched only a moment longer, and Joci saved the day. "Kayden, we're having a big dinner at the house the day after tomorrow to celebrate the end of the Build-Off and we'd love it if you and Dakota would join us. Your dad has already agreed to join us as well. The girls and I will be cooking."

He watched Kayden's gaze rest on each of the women in the family, each waiting for her answer. She smiled the most beautiful smile he'd ever seen. "We'd love to. What can I bring?"

Joci shook her head. "Nothing. You'll be in Sturgis all week working and we're just along for the ride. We enjoy having family dinners and wanted to have one while we're here. Just bring Dakota and we'll enjoy the evening together."

"Thank you very much. We appreciate you including our family."

Dog finished his soda. "Okay, saddle up."

The group finished their drinks and began grabbing money off the bar and generally getting ready to ride.

JT looked over at Oakes. "Are you feeling better today?"

Oakes walked to him and held out his hand. "I'm good and thank you for helping last evening."

"Of course." Leaning in to whisper, he added, "I wish you'd let us help you."

Oakes shook his head. "Nothing to help with, son."

24

The ride to Sturgis was quiet, each lost in thought. Almost there, JT turned to her. "What time are you leaving today? I want to follow you home."

"You do? Why?" The sly smile she turned on him made his nostrils flare. She watched him swallow, then glance out of the corner of his eye. He pulled to a stop at an intersection and leaned toward her just a bit.

"Because earlier was just a warm-up. I've got more playing to do with you and tonight is about the longest I'm willing to wait."

A shiver ran the length of her body and her nipples puckered. He hitched his mouth up on one side.

Since she'd already decided to play with him as much as she could while he was here, she smiled right back at him. As sultry as her voice could be, she ran her fingers from his knee to his thigh, resting her hand high up on his thigh. "That's about as long as I'm willing to wait, too."

His breath hitched. Grabbing her hand, he placed it over the quickly-thickening bulge in his jeans. With a gravelly voice, he managed, "Look what you do to me, Kayd."

She squeezed then pulled her hand away, teasing. "Just you wait to see what I'll do to you."

A horn honking from behind brought his attention to the road and he quickly took off following the Rolling Thunder group as they rode ahead of them into Sturgis.

They parked in the designated spots behind the building where they each had their respective business pursuits going on. Her Jeep was just a few spaces and rows from his truck and trailer. She turned to open her door, then stopped and said, "I'll be ready to go around seven o'clock, will that work?"

He nodded. "Yeah." Hopping from the truck, he walked around to help her down, held her head gently in his hands and kissed her lips softly, but thoroughly. "Have a good day today," he whispered.

"You too. I'll stop around if I can."

He nodded.

J T stood next to his truck as he watched Kayden walk into the building. Dang girl was sexy, and her fine ass swayed as she moved. She was going to be hard to leave behind. He turned his attention to matters at hand. Today they were selecting the top three Build-Off bikes and he hoped to God he was one of them. Several weeks ago, this was all he thought about; now, for some reason, it didn't hold the same appeal it had.

Taking a deep breath, he turned the handle on the door and and stepped into the building. The air conditioner was already working overtime and the building was full of designers. He walked to his stall, uncovered his bike and looked at it once again with a fresh set of eyes. It was still a thing of beauty. Glistening white paint and chrome made it look sleek and sexy. But she was bad ass and he'd had the pleasure of taking her out on the road and working her up to a hundred twenty miles an hour. She was smooth, even at that speed.

The same gravelly-voiced judge who'd been around all week, yelled out, "Doors are opening; get ready, the street's full."

The large double doors leading to the street opened up and the crowds of people came flowing in, each with their entry ballot and a little pencil. They'd walk around and look at each bike, and then place their ballots in the box in front of the stage. Tonight around six o'clock, the organizers would select the top three vote getters. Those three bikes would then be set up on stage and each of the designers would have the chance to tell the crowd all about their bike, start it up, and let the voters decide from there. That was all tomorrow, then the day after, the winner would be announced. Three friggen more days.

He turned his head to the back room where he knew Kayden was selling her clothing and wondered if he'd be able to get the chance to see her in action. She was proud of her clothing and his future sisters-in-law had been oohing and aahing over it for the past couple of days. Ryder mentioned that Molly was sexy as hell in the corset she'd purchased and he thought she should buy a few more.

JT had raised his hand in the air. "No more information, please." He didn't need to think of his future sister-in-law in a sexy corset.

He glanced around at the people walking by and whispering to each other about this and that. No one was looking at him, so he stepped away and walked to the doorway separating the two parts of the building. He glanced across the room and saw Kayden standing behind her table with a dark-haired man standing next to her. They were engaged in conversation and she was showing him different pieces of clothing. What irritated him was the man was behind her table, alongside her and they looked friendly. He said something; she laughed. She said something back; he laughed. He pointed to the back of the room, and she nodded and stepped from behind the table. The man followed her, his hand at the small of her back. The people milling about blocked his view of where they went and his heart began racing, his neck grew tight. It was hard to breathe but he craned his neck to locate them. Not seeing them, he stepped into the room and slowly walked to the back, his eyes peeled for them.

"What the fuck are you doing out here?" Frog, the Rolling Thunder mechanic who was with them this week chided. "People may want to talk to the builder and you know that helps with votes."

JT shook his head to dispel the negative thoughts. "I know. I'm going back right now." He turned to head back to his stall, berating himself for not keeping his head in the game. He'd worked his ass off on this bike for this very event. Focus, dumbass.

The hours ticked by slowly, and JT felt like he'd answered the same five questions over and over, but he smiled and flirted just a little with the ladies, hoping for their votes. Sure, he wanted to win because people thought his bike was the best, but it didn't hurt for the extra fluff vote or two. A sultry blonde with a see-through black lace tank top walked over to him. He'd noticed her walking around before, hard not to with her large breasts almost exposed. Her blood red lips parted and the contrast with her white teeth was almost too much. The thick black liner and long straight hair was a look for a magazine; up close and personal, it was unattractive. Not at all like Kayden.

"What's your name, baby?" she purred.

"JT. Yours?"

She parted her lips in the biggest smile he'd ever seen. It diminished her whole face. "Treasure." She moved her shoulders in an effort to jiggle her breasts. "Nice to meet you. Did you build this beauty?"

He looked down at the bike and nodded. "That I did." He smiled at her. "Are you a model?"

She threw her head back and laughed the phoniest laugh he'd heard, loud enough to capture the attention of many people. Suddenly men were standing all around them, mostly watching the show. She reached up and laid her palm on his chest and whispered, "Built strong and lean, just like I like 'em."

He felt the hair stand on the back of his neck. "You'll have to find your own...Treasure," came the sarcastic remark from Kayden, who'd somehow made her way through the throng of men. She walked up to JT and looked him in the eye. "This one's mine."

A smirk creased his face as he stared into the hazel depths of her eyes and watched her emotions running through them. Damn, she was sexy when she was territorial. So hot!

25

So excited to tell JT what had just happened, Kayden's excitement turned to irritation and then jealousy when she saw the bimbo touching him. She may not have him for long, but she sure as hell wasn't going to share him while she did have him, that was for sure. She pushed and weaved her way through the crowd of mostly men that had formed and stood her ground. She told him with her eyes that she wasn't joking around, that it wasn't funny. Not even a little.

Then, he smirked at her. She fought between anger and melting. He smirked. At. Her. But, dammit, he looked good doing it, too. Treasure walked away with a quick, "You're a lucky lady." JT winked at her and said, "Do you have a minute to wait until I speak to these guys here?"

She nodded and stood to the side, watching him beam over his baby. She saw more than a few guys make notes or vote on their papers and she smiled sweetly at them when they glanced her way. She could work a crowd, too; she'd been doing it for years in the bar. When the last of this group had left, he turned to her and kissed her lips.

"So. I'm yours?" He studied her expression. "That's new."

She touched a couple buttons on his shirt, then looked into his eyes. "I think when you spank a woman, that means she owns you." She slyly smiled at him. "And about that. You always spank your women?"

He shook his head. "I've never spanked anyone before." He leaned down close to her ear. "But I plan on spanking you again." He nuzzled her neck and she heard him breathe deeply into her hair. It was simply exciting the way he seemed to want to breathe in her scent. No one had ever done that before.

A shiver ran through her and she squeezed her legs together. He stepped back. "Now, what about you? I saw you leave with some man; what the fuck was that about?"

She smiled brightly. "I came to tell you. He wants to license Kayden's Concealed Carry. I'm so excited; it's what I've dreamed of."

"License, as in, he'll pay you for your designs and then manufacture them?"

She squealed in delight. "Yes. Isn't that fantastic?"

His smile took her breath away, simply nothing like it in the world. "If that's what you want, it's fantastic." He cocked his head. "Why would you want that?"

She pursed her lips. "The fun part is the creating, designing." She looked at his bike and held her hand out. "What was the fun part of building this bike, creating it or actually manufacturing it?"

He glanced at his bike and nodded. "The creating. Coming up with the different ideas and getting them to come to life."

"Right? Now I can create, draw, design, and pull something together and get paid for it and someone else will go through the trouble of manufacturing it and selling it. It's perfect. I'll be able to support Dakota and myself without the bar."

She threw herself into his arms and hung on. He smelled spicy and delicious and she couldn't wait to get him home and enjoy herself with his body. She hadn't had the time to look at him naked and she wanted to. Badly. Especially after this morning.

~

She landed against his chest and he instinctively wrapped his arms around her and squeezed. She fit perfectly against his body. Her curves molded to him like they'd been made for each other. Watching her excitement at getting a licensing deal made his heart hammer in his chest. They had so much in common with each other. They both had dreams of building their lives in a way that suited them—not settling.

He set her on her feet and looked into the hazel depths, noting the brown flecks that gave them the deepness in color but the green hues that gave her the exotic edge he'd first found so damn sexy. He leaned in and softly kissed her lips, his hand holding her head in place until he was ready to release her. She whimpered and he caught it in his mouth and growled. When he ended the kiss he watched her slowly open her eyes, seductive she was. Damn.

"Don't leave here without me. Hear?"

Smiling, she shrugged a shoulder. "Or what?"

He swatted her ass, eliciting a yelp. "More of that."

"That's not going to make me behave."

He grinned. "Then, let's say this. If you leave without me, there will be no spanking. Yeah?"

She giggled and walked toward her end of the building, glancing back at him once and winking, which made his cock thicken and butterflies swirl in his stomach. Wench.

26

The announcements rang out through the PA system. "Five minutes and the top three Build-Off bikes will be selected. Come see who the top three builders are this year at the main building in front of the stage. Five minutes."

JT glanced at Ryder and Gunnar and let out a long breath. "This is it guys; my moment of truth."

Gunnar lightly punched his shoulder. "You've got this, bro. There's a fair amount of competition here, but you've got this."

JT nodded. "Where's Dad?"

Ryder pointed to the stage. "Already there and he's rooting for you, JT. Despite his reservations about you moving into building, he's proud of you."

JT swallowed. "I sure as hell hope so. I've been railing on him pretty hard these past couple of months. We've never argued so much. I know he was worried and it affects the business, but I needed him to see I could do this."

Gunnar chuckled. "He sees it."

The announcer stood at the front of the stage. "Are we ready to hear who this year's top three builders are?"

The crowd yelled and whistled.

"Don't forget, tomorrow is the only day to vote for the number one bike. Four hours only, from ten o'clock in the morning until two in the afternoon. After that, it's all over. So, get your asses out of bed, hear me?"

The crowd cheered and laughed. In Sturgis the parties ran well into the night and the town didn't get hopping until around ten o'clock or later depending on the doings the night before.

JT nodded at his brothers and the three of them made their way to the Rolling Thunder group near the front of the stage. Joci hugged him and yelled over the crowd to be heard, "I'm so proud of you, JT. We both are."

She looked at Jeremiah and he grabbed JT's shoulders and pulled him in for a hug. "Your mom's right. We're both proud of you."

Choked up, all he could do was swallow. He looked around for Kayden; he hoped she'd be here. With all of the people standing around, she could be anywhere, but he wanted to see her. She'd calm his damn churning stomach.

The announcer revved the crowd. "Okay, are you all ready for the first builder?"

The crowd yelled and cheered.

"These builders are not announced in any particular order. The first builder is from the Midwest. He's worked in the family business most of his life. This bike is the first bike he's built on his own."

JT swallowed, his heart pounded so hard he thought he'd lose consciousness.

"Come on up here, Gene Raymond."

The crowd went wild with excitement. JT's stomach dropped. He'd thought it was him; shit, he needed to get a handle on this. His knees were shaking and he couldn't help it, and he continued looking around for Kayden.

The announcer continued. "Our next builder is also from the Midwest. He's been building bikes for many years with his father and brother. He's a veteran of Operation Enduring Freedom, proudly serving in the United States Marine Corps. This isn't his first time here, but it is his first time as the sole builder. Come on up, JT Sheppard."

His family and co-workers around him all jostled and hugged, yelling loudly and slapping him on the back. His dad squeezed his shoulders and JT looked into his eyes. They were glistening with unshed tears. Jeremiah gave him a little push toward the stage, and JT made his way through the throngs of people who thunked him on the back and congratulated him. He walked up the five steps to stand on the stage and he couldn't help himself, he looked around for her. Where was she? He glanced around the crowd, wanting to see that she was here watching him reach one of his goals. He swallowed the lump in his throat and tried to tamp down the disappointment that she wasn't interested in him as any more than a sexual partner. He waved his hand to the crowd, raising the noise level to deafening. He smiled his brightest smile.

The announcer barked out. "This is it. Our final builder completing the top three. Are you ready?"

JT barely heard the announcer as he continued on, then he saw her—right at the front of the stage—jostled and pushed by the horde of bikers, most dressed in leather vests with varying patches signifying their affiliations to various clubs, groups, and organizations. His eyes met hers and his heart sped up at the sight. Her alluring smile challenged the shine of the sun glinting off the chrome on his bike. She blew him a kiss, and that was it. His eyes welled up and he swallowed furiously to get control of his emotions. He pointed at her and winked. He motioned to her to go to the steps leading to the stage.

The announcer walked over to him, and stepped between him and Kayden and began asking him questions. JT had to listen carefully to hear his questions above the deafening noise.

27

S he knew that she'd never felt like this about any man before, and that was saying something. She thought about him all the time lately, wanted to share things with him about her day or her life. Today when she'd been offered the licensing deal, the only thing she wanted to do was run and tell JT. She laid her hand against her stomach and drowned out all of the noise going on around her. She vaguely heard JT answer mundane questions from the announcer but her mind reeled at what this meant.

She was pulled into a hug by two squealing women, who were jumping and laughing. Molly and Emma jostled her around in their excitement.

Molly's dark shiny hair swung as she yelled, "Isn't this exciting?"

Kayden only nodded in response.

Emma clasped her hands over Kayden's. "This is so awesome. It's all he's thought about for the past two or three months. All the boys have discussed this day until we were sick of the conversation."

More of the Rolling Thunder group joined them at the bottom of the steps, including Jeremiah and Joci. Once again, the crowd roared and Kayden looked up to see JT leaving the stage waving and walking toward her. Her heart pounded and she was on the verge of tears when he scooped her up in his arms and spun her around—his embrace so tight she couldn't breathe. He whispered in her ear, "Thank you for coming to see this. It means more than you know."

She wrapped her arms around his neck and whispered back, "Oh, I know and congratulations."

He set her on her feet and was engulfed by his family in hugs and thumps on his back. She was pushed along with them as they made their way toward the doors. Unable to break away and not sure what to do, Kayden allowed herself to move along with them and out into the fresh, sultry air. The noise wasn't as deafening and she felt like she could breathe again, despite the heat. His arm wrapped around her shoulders and pulled her close. The clean scent of his aftershave and the feel of his body pushed against hers was exhilarating. Despite the ninety plus degrees, she didn't want him to let go.

He kissed the side of her head and tears sprang to her eyes. She swiped at them without thought.

A soft sweet voice broke into her emotional turmoil. "Kayden?"

She blinked and concentrated on Joci. "We'd love to toast JT's achievement. Would you be able to join us?"

Plastering on a smile, she replied, "Of course. It isn't every day two momentous occasions occur; we certainly should celebrate."

Joci cocked her head. "Two?"

JT proudly exclaimed, "Kayd got a licensing deal for her concealed carry clothing today, Mom."

More congratulations from these people who were fast becoming a new family to her. Emma hugged her. "That's just fantastic, Kayden. You must be so proud."

Kayden embraced Emma and whispered, "Thank you, Emma; I'm so happy right now, I'm afraid I'm a bit of a mess."

Jeremiah stepped forward. "Congratulations, you two. It seems as though we have two reasons to celebrate tonight." To Kayden, he asked, "Does your dad have a bartender at OK's?"

Nodding, she answered, "He does all this week."

Jeremiah turned to their group. "Okay, saddle up, we'll head to OK's for drinks."

〜

His dad had told him he fell in love with Joci the day he met her, it just took a little while for his brain to realize it. Driving behind Kayden's Jeep, he could see the back of her head just above the top of her seat, her messy do moving as the wind from the open windows blew it to and fro. In moments of reflection, and he'd had a few as his dad and then his brothers fell in love, he wondered if a woman would ever capture his attention like the new women in his family had caught his dad and brothers. He'd doubted it as he'd been through a fair amount of women, and they had just seemed like fluff and fodder. The woman he dared to dream about would have to be a good mother to their future children. She'd need to understand that sometimes his brain wandered as he was pulling together his next big design for a bike, component, or gadget. A sense of humor was a must and she'd need to understand that he and his family were close and so important to him and they would need to get along. And while looks aren't everything, an attraction was a must. It also would be a bonus if she wanted him as much as he wanted her. Big bonus.

He let his mind wander so much for the remainder of the ride that he was surprised as they drove into Shady Pines and the quaint little town passed by his windows. Taking a deep breath, he blinked the dryness from his eyes and focused on the little white Jeep in front of him again. As they left town behind, the buildings turned to green grass, gravel driveways and then the little park with the colorful playground equipment. Finally, the parking lot to OK Leathers Saloon. She turned into the parking lot and continued on behind the building and then to her garage, the door already opening. He followed her through the parking lot and parked in front of the garage door, knowing what it looked like, but he didn't care.

She jumped from her Jeep, her sexy legs exposed between her boots and her skirt. He admired them as she walked, then his vision focused on the ample breasts swaying slightly as she strode purposefully toward him. Yum.

He continued his perusal and gazed into her eyes, and his heart sped.

As she reached him, she wrapped her arms around his neck and consumed his lips as if she were starving. Her breasts pressed into his chest caused his jeans to grow tight. His arms snaked around her waist and pulled her closer, his hands floating down her body and grabbing her sweet tight ass and wrenched her closer to the hardness behind his zipper. When she whimpered, a jolt ran through him and his heart hammered.

She pulled her head back and looked into his eyes. Her voice was soft and seductive. "I can wait for this for about an hour, then I don't think I'll have any self-control. How about you?"

Well, fuck me. She'd make him cum right here and now. "An hour?" He nipped her lips lightly one more time and squeezed her tighter to him. "I was hoping for less." He ground his hardness into her. "But if you can hold out for an hour, I can too."

28

Kayden sat at a bar-top table by the front window with Emma, Molly, and Joci while the men hovered around the bar and the pool table. The women chattered about Molly and Ryder's upcoming wedding. It was sort of bittersweet. She was beginning to like these women so damn much. She wouldn't be there for the wedding and to see how happy Molly and Ryder were on the day they joined as man and wife. It stabbed her heart to think of it.

Her hands laid on the top of the table, folded together as she stared out the window at the picnic tables out front that she'd so painstakingly cleaned and decorated last week. Sturgis week was their biggest week of the year and she'd wanted things perfect. Now, her life was going in a different direction and she was going to need to tell her father that they should sell the bar and move on. She dreaded that conversation. Disappointing her father left a bitter taste in her mouth.

Soft hands squeezed hers. "Hey there, did you hear me?"

Kayden looked into Molly's smiling blue eyes. "I'm so sorry; my mind was wandering." She smiled brightly and admonished herself for ignoring these wonderful women who'd only been nice to her.

"I said, I would absolutely love it if you would make my wedding dress. I love the corset I purchased from you. Ryder does, too." She glanced at Emma, then back to Kayden. "Emma and I were talking and we thought you could design one for me in white and we could have a detachable skirt added to it so I could also wear it for Ryder on our wedding night. I'm not going to tell him; it'll be a surprise."

Kayden's eyebrows rose into her bangs. Another pierce to her heart. She swallowed the excitement laced with disappointment. "Wow. I've never designed a wedding dress before, but I've always wanted to."

Molly beamed. "I know it's not a ton of time, but I can sew and so can Emma and we'll do what we can to help out. We have three months."

Kayden calculated how much work would go into the actual designing. "I'm hesitant to commit because I don't know how quickly this licensing deal will come through and how much of my time it will consume."

Molly pleaded, "Will you just think about it?"

Hard to deny her smiling hopeful face, Kayden nodded. "Yes, I can promise I'll think about it."

Now Kayden's mind wandered to designing a wedding dress and she had to admit, the ideas were flying through her brain at the speed of light.

～

As the Rolling Thunder group roared from the parking lot, Kayden brought the empty glasses from the tables to the bar. Tim, the part-time bartender smiled and said, "Go on home Kayden, I've got this."

She smiled at him and looked around the bar. There were patrons in the bar tonight; It wasn't full, but nicely filled and she felt hopeful things would be okay in their lives again. Even though the bar would have to go, they just might get lucky and make a little money until they sold it.

JT stood and she turned to look into his eyes. They'd been apart since entering the bar. The women had commandeered the table she'd just cleared and the men congregated around the bar and pool table. She glanced over at him often though, and he'd always been watching her. Every time their eyes met, the jolt screamed through her body and caused her to squirm. He was without a doubt the sexiest and most intriguing man she'd ever met—he made her feel everything good.

Looking over at Tim, she said, "Thanks, Tim."

JT reached forward and took her hand in his, leading them through the kitchen and out the back door. As they stepped outside, he pulled her closer and wrapped his arm around her shoulders. The thrill of being this close to him made her knees weak.

29

Entering Kayden's apartment above the garage gave him a thrill. Something about being in her space, smelling her scent in every room and seeing her personal touches on each surface made him feel connected to her on a different level. She set her keys and purse on the table and silently took his hand and drew him to the back of the apartment. His vision focused on her back, encased in that sexy black blouse, hugging her tightly, her shape was of the perfect motorcycle. Her ass the back fender, the narrow waist, the seat and the sweep of her back the gas tank. The visions of him riding her again and again filled his mind and his arousal went full blown.

She glanced back at him, and the seductive look she trained on him made his hands shake. When they stepped into her bedroom, she released his hand and walked to the nightstand. She picked up a small device, swiped and tapped, and the room filled with the music of "Tennessee Whiskey", the song he'd first heard as he walked into the bar and saw her standing there. She turned and began unbuttoning her blouse, stepping toward him. "That first day, when you walked into the bar and this song was playing? I'll never forget it. I downloaded it that night and I've listened to it over and over again, remembering you walking up to me." Her voice was husky and sexy.

Each button exposed a bit more of her skin and his mouth went dry. Her eyes never left his and his heart beat out a rhythm that could rival the thump of a motor at one hundred miles per hour. She undid the last button and slowly pulled her blouse from her shoulders and dropped it to the floor. The little black lacey bra she wore allowed him to see through the lace and the pretty pink nipples hiding behind.

Her mouth hitched up on one side as she watched him look at her. He saw the little clasp between her breasts and reached a finger under it and popped it forward, releasing her gorgeous breasts into his waiting hands. He quickly massaged and squeezed his new toys with abandon. Dipping his head, he laved each breast in turn with his tongue, sucking a nipple into his mouth and gently biting down until she whimpered. The saltiness of her skin added to the sensations of her slippery nipples teasing his mouth, and he worried he'd lose all control. Her hands drove into his hair and clenched, holding on tight.

He stood and watched her face as her eyes slowly opened. His voice was gruff and tight with need. "Take the rest off. I want to watch you."

She seductively smiled at him and gently pushed on the middle of his chest until he plopped down on the foot of the bed. She took two steps back and slowly unsnapped her skirt, gingerly lowering the zipper. She pulled it open to reveal one of her concealed carry belts. The bright pink trim formed a V and pointed in the direction he was interested in at this moment. She shimmied her skirt down and tossed it aside. Unfastening each hook and eye took more time but he watched her breasts sway and jiggle, the dampness from his mouth still glistening as the soft light from the window touched them. Dropping her belt, all that was left was a tiny scrap of black lace that she quickly wiggled out of, and completely naked, she was magnificent. She stepped toward him and tugged on his t-shirt, pulling it up and over his head.

"I've thought of this all day," she huskily whispered.

His t-shirt sailed away and her hands touched his bare skin, leaving a tingling trail behind every inch she touched. The electricity flowing through his body at her contact took his breath away. She paused as she touched the various tattoos on his arms and across his chest, signifying his love of his unit in the Marines, the 1st Combat Engineer Battalion. She admired his ink, his physique, and his body as she lovingly roved her hands over every exposed inch of him. She softly cupped his face in her hands and whispered, "You're beautiful, JT. I love your body."

He huffed out a breath and swallowed. "You're the most beautiful woman I've ever seen, Kayden, and I want you so bad, I think I'm going to combust."

She leaned down and lightly kissed his lips. "We can't have you combusting until you're inside of me."

Zing. Right. To. His. Cock. He jerked open his jeans, laid back on the bed, grabbed a condom from his pocket and pushed them down his hips. Kayden helped him by pulling the jeans from his legs, then quickly pulling his briefs from his hips and sliding them down his legs. She slowly ran her hands up his legs, stopping to lick the length of his cock, causing it to jerk and pre-cum to form at the tip. With a light touch of her finger, she swirled the pearl of moisture around the tip of it and smiled as she continued up his body and positioned herself over him. She took the condom from his fingers and ripped open the package. He felt paralyzed as he watched her seductive motions, willing to wait to see what this sexy siren would do to him next. So far, it was beyond anything he'd ever experienced before.

She took his cock in her hands, gently pumping it and admiring it with her soft touches and squeezes. She placed the condom on top and rolled it with her fingers, lovingly covering him. She reared up and placed him at her entrance, notching him just inside. She looked into his eyes as she slowly slid down on him and his heart roared. His hands gripped her hips tightly but he was unable to look away from her. As she rose and lowered, the sway of her breasts in his peripheral vision was a sight he wanted to remember forever. Imprinting this moment into his brain was tantamount to your first ride on your first bike. Unforgettable!

He held her tightly as he helped her raise and lower herself on him; the feeling of her lips hugging and sucking him in took his breath away. And as great as all of this was, the moment she threw her head back and her face took on the intoxicating expression of passion as her orgasm raced through her something happened, neurons fired like pistons on a racing engine. His vision dimmed and he tumbled over the edge with her.

30

K ayden crawled up the bed, pulling the covers back and lying on the pillows against the headboard. She was in so much trouble here. This man was everything she could ever hope for, but he would be leaving soon and she would be broken into thousands of pieces. Why did life have to be so damn hard?

JT returned from the bathroom, striding through the door in all of his glorious awesomeness and she thrilled at the simplicity of him filling the space in her bedroom. His body was a work of art—literally. The tattoos across his chest and on his upper arms were beautiful depictions of his time in Afghanistan and the love he had for his brothers-at-arms. She knew how strong that bond was; her father had carried it for more than thirty years. JT's dad was one of those bond-brothers. Weird how life worked out.

As he climbed into the bed beside her, his scent enveloped her as his strong arms pulled her into his side. She thought about resisting, but seriously, how stupid would that be? She had so little time with him. She rested in the crook of his arm, her cheek against his chest, the hairs on his chest tickling her nose. She lovingly brushed her fingertips across his taut skin, swirling around the puckered disks and sliding lower and back up again. After two or three times, his husky voice broke her trance. "You keep going lower, and we're going in for round two."

She giggled. "I think it would be round three for today."

He lifted his head to look down at her, then chuckled. "I'm ready if you are."

"I think it would be hard not to be ready for you, JT." She twisted in his arm and laid half of her body on his, resting her chin on her hand so it didn't poke into him. "I think watching you leave will be the hardest thing I've ever done."

She could feel his heart beat ratchet up, and he gazed into her eyes. "Yeah, I've thought the same thing."

She reached her arm up to smooth the wrinkle on his forehead and brush strands of hair from his brow. He grabbed her arm and looked at the tattoo inscription on the inside of her wrist. *I'll love you always. Mom.*

When he spoke, his voice was gruff. "Tell me about this."

She took a deep breath and rolled to her back, holding up her wrist to read the inscription. "That's my mom's signature from the last birthday card she ever gave me." She smiled, remembering that day. "I turned twelve and I had my eyes on the most beautiful pair of cowgirl boots I'd ever seen. Timmy Bristol's dad made the best boots around. He tanned the hides right in the back of the shop." She looked at him. "Timmy goes by Tim now, and he was tending bar today."

Pushing herself back into the pillows in a sitting position, she continued, "Anyway, my mom was a free spirit. She didn't believe in belongings or being tied to 'things' and she thought my obsession with those boots was unhealthy. I never dreamed she'd get them for me. Dad was drinking a lot back then and he didn't even know I wanted them. He was so inebriated most days." She felt the bed dip and turned to see JT had turned on his side, lying with his head propped up on his hand, watching her.

"So, the morning of my birthday, I got up and I was afraid to be excited. My birthday presents usually revolved around taking a hike and finding a new flower or feeding chipmunks in the woods or going to Custer National Park and watching the baby buffalos play; I never knew what it would be. She didn't like making schedules or keeping appointments. She said it interfered with her 'peace.'

"I got out of bed, showered, and dressed casually in denim shorts and a tank and quietly walked into the living room. There on the coffee table sat my brand new boots with the prettiest orange flower sitting on the toe and a card next to them. The card was handmade from a grocery bag—we never wasted anything—and all it said was *Happy Birthday. I'll Love You Always. Mom.*"

She swiped at the irritating tear that slid down her cheek. JT reached up and gently ran his thumb under her eye, collecting another tear.

"I wore those boots until they were clear wore out—scuffed, battered, and didn't fit anymore. But they meant the world to me, especially because she died three weeks later."

She glanced at JT. "They were the last gift I'd gotten that I never dreamed I'd get. I saved that grocery bag card and still have it. I took it to a tattoo shop in Sturgis before I left for college so I'd have her with me always and he duplicated her signature on my wrist. I look at it when I need her peacefulness inside me."

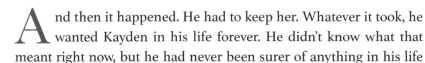

And then it happened. He had to keep her. Whatever it took, he wanted Kayden in his life forever. He didn't know what that meant right now, but he had never been surer of anything in his life —even knowing he could win the Biker Build-Off.

"Is that why your logo for Kayden's Concealed Carry is an orange flower?" he asked.

She softly replied, "Yeah."

He watched her swallow to keep her emotions in check. So many years had passed and still she was affected by those few moments that meant so much. She lightly fingered his hair and smoothed his brow with her thumb. "I sign every one of Dakota's cards—which I make by hand—with *I'll love you always, Kota*." She let out a breath. "I want her to always have that from me."

He leaned forward and lightly kissed her lips, running his thumb over her cheek and sliding his hand into her hair. Moments in time can imprint themselves on your mind; this day, this time, these moments were forever imprinted on his.

Rising over her, he reached behind her back and slowly pulled her down to a lying position. He consumed her lips, savored the taste of her sweetness. His tongue sought to touch every surface of her mouth. She wrapped her arms around him and held tight and his heart burst. He gently slid himself inside of her and moaned with her when they both felt the erotic sensations of joining together—heart and soul.

He moved in and out of her, savoring the feel of what her body did to his. He watched her eyes deepen in color from the greenish hue they usually held to the deeper color of warm chocolate. When she stared into his eyes like she was committing him to memory, it made him feel like climbing right inside of her and never leaving.

He pumped into her with more urgency, needing to leave an imprint on her. His muscles tightened as he increased his pace and a smile grew on her face, urging him on. Her moans of pleasure were better than the music still playing from the speaker and her increased breathing alerted him she was close.

He thrust forward several times more and as soon as he saw her mouth open in ecstasy, he spilled into her as he continued to push himself as far in as he could go.

He cradled her in his arms and he kept himself on his elbows so as not to crush her, breathing in her hair, her skin, and their unique scent together.

She squeezed her arms around him, holding him just as close and he reveled in the feel of her pulling him to her.

From the kitchen, a cell phone rang, muffled by the confines of her purse. He groaned and raised his head to look into her eyes. "Do you need to get that?"

Her lips spread across her face in a straight line. "Yes. It might be Payton needing something for Dakota."

He rolled off her and she rose to a sitting position. She turned to look at him. "We didn't use a condom."

"I know." He met her gaze.

"JT..." The phone began ringing again.

Taking a deep breath, she stood and silently walked from the bedroom, her spine straight, her ass perfection.

31

K ayden used the bathroom to clean up then padded quietly to the kitchen, rummaged in her purse and pulled out her phone. Three missed calls, all from Payton. Worry creasing her brow, she quickly dialed Payton and looked out the window facing the bar to see how busy it was out there.

"Kayden, thank God you called back. Where are you?"

Tamping down the panic rising to the surface, she said, "I'm home. What's wrong?"

Payton began crying. "I'm on my way to the hospital. Duncan..." She sobbed and tried to speak again. "Duncan was shot today. I'm on my way to the hospital. The kids are with my neighbor, but it will be much easier if you are able to pick up Dakota."

Kayden heard her friend sobbing and tears sprang to her eyes. "Oh, Payton. Honey, I'm so, so sorry." Swallowing to keep her emotions in check, she continued, "Do you know how bad?"

"No. They only said...I needed to... get...get to the hospital...right away." She broke down crying.

"Okay, listen. You focus on your driving; I'll get the kids. It's going to be okay, Payton."

She continued to listen to her friend cry as she ran to the bedroom. JT had gotten up and already had his jeans on and was pulling on a t-shirt when she entered.

Rifling through her drawers for clothing, she continued holding the phone to her ear. Finally, Payton regained control of herself and said, "My mom's coming for the kids, so don't worry about Catcher and Ruby. I'll call you as soon as I know anything."

"Honey, do you need me there with you?" Her voice broke and she stopped so she wouldn't set Payton off again.

"Thanks, Kayd, but let me get there and see what I'm dealing with. Duncan's parents are on the way, too."

"Okay. I love you, Payton. I'll talk to you later."

With shaking hands, she set her phone on the dresser and turned to JT. She broke down as soon as his arms encircled her. He held her tight and the comfort he provided was immeasurable. As soon as she could, she told him what happened. "I have to go and get Dakota. Depending on how shaken up she is, I'll go to the hospital."

"I'll drive you." The gruffness in his voice was soothing.

"I don't want to burden you JT."

"Nope. You shouldn't drive as shaken up as you are, and if Dakota needs you to hold her, you can't while you're driving." He kissed her forehead. "Get dressed. I'll go and unhook the trailer."

She nodded and watched his face for any signs of irritation, but what she saw was concern, and maybe...love. Hopefully...love.

"I never would have thought being a park ranger would get a person shot. She didn't know any other details?" JT watched the road as he drove, but firmly held onto Kayden's hand as they made their way to Payton's.

"No, they must have just called her and told her to go to the hospital." She squeezed his hand. "Right here on the left. The little tan house."

He turned the truck into the driveway and put it in park. He opened his door and looked back at Kayden when she hadn't moved. His brows rose. "What?"

She pursed her lips, but said, "Nothing."

She opened her door and they walked together to Mrs. Harris' front door. Kayden pointed to their right. "That's Duncan and Payton's house." The brick ranch with the little overhang over the porch and sidewalk looked inviting. Two white rocking chairs and a little table in between them sat on the porch, beckoning a person to come and sit a spell.

Kayden knocked on the door and a tiny white haired lady with a floral blouse in a myriad of types and colors and blue capris opened the door. Her smiled widened and she immediately reached up to hug Kayden and pat her on the back. She looked back at the door and then turned to Kayden. "The kids don't know anything. Payton told them she had an appointment and she ushered them over here quickly and quietly. We've been making cookies, which pleases all of them, including Ed."

Her white head turned to JT and she glanced between him and Kayden. Kayden chuckled, and said, "Doris, this is JT. I'll bet you remember Dad talking about Dog from his war days. Dog is JT's father and they're here for Sturgis." Kayden smiled up at him.

Doris beamed. "It's nice to meet you; come on in out of the heat, you two." She opened the door, and the first thing he noticed was the yummy smell of fresh baked chocolate chip cookies. Then came the giggles and chatter of little voices and the slower replies from a voice clearly aged by years and life. Doris led them through the living room into the kitchen as she proudly proclaimed, "Kota honey, look who came to pick you up."

Dakota's beaming little face landed on her mom and then JT. Suddenly he was nervous about her reaction to him. She jumped up from her chair at the table and squealed, "Mommy!" as she ran and threw herself into Kayden's waiting arms. He watched as Kayden peppered her daughter's little face with kisses and the little girl giggled and squirmed.

Kayden set her down and she immediately looked up at JT and said. "Hi, JT. How did you know I was here?"

JT knelt down and said, "Payton called your mommy and told her. It smells like you've been making something very delicious."

Nodding her little blonde head, she giggled. "We're making cookies. I get to put the dough on the sheet. Ruby gets to put a M&M on them and Chance gets to carry the sheet to the oven for Mrs. Harris."

Grinning at her exuberance, he replied, "It sounds like you're all helping Mrs. Harris out a lot."

"We are. Except Mr. Harris keeps eating them."

They all laughed and Mr. Harris held his hand out to shake JT's. "Name's Ed."

JT leaned down and shook Ed's hand. He was a frail little man sitting in a wheelchair parked at the end of the kitchen table. His eye were blue, but the color had begun to fade with the years. His small bony hand still had a firm grip and his smile was friendly. "JT."

"Mr. Harris, JT comes from Wisc...Wis..." Tilting her head, Dakota looked at JT. "What do you call it?"

JT chuckled. "Wisconsin."

Dakota nodded her head, pleased he got it right. He couldn't help but laugh; she was simply adorable. Maddy would be this age in no time.

"JT, you and Mommy need to have a cookie before Mr. Harris eats them all. Mrs. Harris said sometimes she can't keep up." Her little hands held up a cookie for him and he took the warm gooey cookie and bit into it. Looking at each of the kids, he said, "You guys did a great job on these cookies. Best I ever had, but don't tell my mom that."

All three little people giggled and nodded. Kayden introduced JT to Chance and Ruby and then the kids got back to making more cookies. Mr. Harris pulled his chair away from the table and looked at Kayden. "Do you know anything more?" He asked quietly.

Kayden shook her head no and Ed nodded to the living room. He glanced back at Doris and she nodded at his quiet communication.

Ed rolled into the living room and Kayden and JT followed. Ed turned his wheelchair around and motioned with his hand for them to sit on the sofa. They did as he asked, sitting close to each other.

Kayden leaned forward, her forearms on her knees, her fingers laced together. Quietly, she asked, "Did Payton tell you about the drugs they found in the park the other night?"

Ed's lips pursed, his brows furrowed and he nodded slightly. "Damn dealers have been moving into this area more and more for a while now—the last couple of years, at least. I had no damned idea it wasn't just the dealers, but the growers, too. Damn it all anyway." His voice was weak and soft but he looked to the kitchen anyway, making sure little ears weren't listening. All that was heard was more giggles and Ruby saying, "No, Chance, I get to put the MM's on."

Kayden smiled. "I think that's what happened to Duncan. She was worried about that this morning when I talked to her, but neither of us actually believed it would happen." She shook her head. "This place is going to hell fast."

"How's your dad doing, Kayden?" Ed asked.

Kayden looked up into JT's eyes and he reached for her hand. He needed the comfort of touching her as much as she seemed to need him. Looking back to Ed, she responded, "He's fine. Stubborn and not telling us the truth; that's for certain."

Ed looked into JT's eyes. He fought against squirming under the man's perusal, then Ed nodded slightly. "Oakes just better watch out. Those damned Devils are involved in this; I just know it."

Kayden's head popped up and she squeezed JT's hand. "Why do you think that?"

"Just do. They've been running into town more and they sure as hell haven't made it a secret around here that they want your place. If I were you all, I'd pack up and run from this place as quick as I could with that little peanut of yours."

Kayden rose quickly and paced to the window. She'd put on a pair of denim shorts with frayed edges and a loose fitting orange tank top. She shouldn't hide that figure from anyone, but he was glad she did. He wanted it all for himself. She looked out the window, and then back to JT. "We should go; I'd like to run by the hospital and see Payton."

JT stood and shook Ed's hand. "It's a pleasure to meet you, Ed."

32

JT and Kayden helped Dakota into the back of his truck. Kayden had gone into Payton's garage and got the extra car seat that Chance had used. She'd never get Dakota into her old car seat again after letting her use Chance's booster. She'd been begging for a booster for some time now, but Kayden didn't have a ton of money, and she'd hoped to hold off on it for a little while longer.

JT had set the booster up behind the passenger seat. Once he had it all arranged and tightened down, he stepped back and let Kayden help Dakota into the truck. She sat in the booster and giggled. "This is really neat," she said. Kayden closed the door and climbed into the front seat. "Mommy, I can see good out the window and it's cooler. I'm not sweaty in here."

She was certainly a happy little gal. He turned to look at Kayden. "What do you want to do?" When her shoulders fell, he reached over and squeezed the back of her neck. "Hey." When she looked up, he said, "I have an idea. How about I take Dakota up to the house with my mom and sisters? You go see Payton and call me when you're done and I'll bring her home. Your dad is probably resting anyway. Deal?"

"I wanna go to the house. Can I, Mommy?"

He watched her process his offer. He quietly said, "It's okay, Angel." Her hazel eyes now looked more amber than the brown from earlier, but still so damned sexy. It was now about eight o'clock in the evening and close to Dakota's bedtime. Since he'd never helped a little person get ready for bed, it scared the shit out of him, but he thought his mom and the girls could sure help if need be.

"You sure?"

"Yeah. I'll drop you off to pick up your Jeep." He gave her neck a reassuring squeeze and she nodded her head. Her hair had been pulled up into a messy whatever they called it. She was stunning even with the faint worry lines around her mouth.

He pulled into her driveway and she pulled her keys from her purse. She turned to look back at Dakota. "You behave for JT, Mrs. Sheppard, and the others; you hear me?"

"I will. I'm always good."

Smiling, she said, "I know you are, Kota. Okay, love you always and I'll see you in just a little bit. Okay?"

Dakota bobbed her head. "Okay. Love you always."

JT looked back at Dakota. "I'll be right back, okay? I just want to make sure Mommy gets inside all right."

"Okay."

He smiled at her. Cute. He glanced at Kayden and hopped from the truck. He followed her into the garage, and as soon as they stepped into the service door, he wrapped her in a hug. He kissed the top of her head and murmured. "It'll be okay, and I hope Duncan is going to be just fine."

She pulled back and kissed his lips. "Take care of my little girl."

He touched his lips to hers and stepped back. As she turned to climb into her Jeep, he swatted her on the ass. She turned, a sexy smile on her face. He shrugged. "Couldn't help myself."

He climbed back into his truck and backed up just a bit. Waiting for Kayden to open the garage door, he looked back at Dakota. "Your mom didn't say you couldn't have ice cream, did she?"

Dakota's eyes lit up and the smile she beamed at him was blinding. "Really?" she squealed.

"Really. We'll go to the store and pick up a big bucket and take it back to the house and share it with everyone. What do you say to that?"

She clapped her hands and squirmed in her booster. "I love chocolate. Can we get chocolate?"

"It's my favorite, too," he said as he noticed the garage door opening. He put his truck in gear and moved out of the way, but waited at the edge of the driveway until she pulled out and closed the door.

"Why do you have to wait for Mommy?"

He looked into the rearview mirror. "I want to make sure she's safe."

"Oh."

Kayden pulled out of the garage and waved at them as she preceded them from the driveway and out onto the main road. She turned in the opposite direction they had to take, so he didn't think she'd be any the wiser until Dakota told her they had ice cream. JT turned toward town and easily found a parking space in front of the grocery store, which was still called 'The General Store.' It fit. The outside was sided with cedar planks which gave it the old western feel. It seemed all of the stores in this town had tried to keep the look and feel alive. It gave Shady Pines the uniqueness that drew people here. JT walked around the back of the truck and opened the door for Dakota. He lifted her from the big truck and took her hand as they walked into the store. He looked down at her. "Is this where you and Mommy shop?"

She nodded her little blonde head. "Yep."

"Do you know where the ice cream is?"

"Yep." She led him to the freezer section and clapped her hands when he pulled out a five-quart bucket of chocolate ice cream. They checked out their purchase and loaded back up.

On the way to the house, Dakota asked, "How come you have so much stuff in your truck?"

He glanced into the rearview mirror and then back to the road. "What kind of stuff do you mean?"

"You have tools and stuff like Grandpa. But Grandpa doesn't keep his in his truck."

He chuckled. "Oh. Well, this isn't my truck; it's my dad's. But it's also the work truck this week, so that's why we have all the tools in it."

"Okay." She looked out the window.

JT kept glancing into the mirror, watching her. She seemed perfectly comfortable and happy.

"Can I have two bowls of ice cream if I eat the first one?"

He chuckled. "We'll see, okay?"

"Okay."

He turned the truck into the driveway of the house. Parking the truck, he followed the same routine, helping Dakota from the truck. He grabbed the ice cream from the passenger floor and took her hand to walk into the house. The sun was close to setting and the sky was colored purple. Hearing a truck driving down the private road caused JT to stop and look down the steep hill to the road. The truck drove past the driveway to the house. It was the first time he'd seen a truck other than theirs on the road since he'd been here.

"Hey, that's Grandpa's truck," Dakota said as she turned her head to watch the truck pass by.

"Are you sure?"

"Yep."

JT watched the truck slow down a short distance down the road and make a right turn. "Who lives down there, do you know?"

"No one lives there. Grandpa just goes there sometimes, but I'm not supposed to tell anyone."

JT squatted in front of her. "How do you know that, Dakota?"

"Umm."

"It's okay. I'm Grandpa's friend. If he needs help, we all want to help him."

She nodded her head. "He takes me there sometimes, but I have to stay in the truck and he goes in the trees and comes out with a bag."

"Thank you for telling me. Shall we go and have some ice cream?"

She squealed and jumped. "Yes, please."

33

Kayden found herself driving up to the house instead of going home. She couldn't bear going in alone right now; she just needed to talk to JT. Driving down the gravel road to the house, she looked up the large hill to see the house lit up at every window. She sighed. It was the perfect house. The cedar siding was stained a medium brown and brought out the richness of the wood. The many windows let the light in and broke up the long lines of the siding. Stuck up in the middle of the hill, it looked like it was tucked into a cozy blanket for a long nap. Turning onto the driveway and making her way up the drive, she rotated her shoulders and suppressed a yawn. Was she getting older, or were the days suddenly becoming overwhelming?

She parked next to the truck and walked to the door. Now she was flummoxed because she didn't know if she should knock or just walk in. Knocking seemed the wiser choice. She waited only a second or two and the door sprung open, and there stood Ryder with a grin on his face.

He held his finger to his lips as a gesture of silence and stepped aside for her to walk in. She entered the media room/bar and noticed that one of the six recliners in the room was tilted back and a blonde head was visible from the back. Ryder motioned her forward and she slowly walked around the theater chairs and her heart raced at the vision before her.

JT was laid back and sleeping in the recliner, and tucked into his arms was Dakota, sleeping peacefully, a soft endearing expression on her face. A faint ring of chocolate rimmed her lips, and her little red cowboy boots were on the floor next to JT's biker boots alongside the chair.

Tears sprang to Kayden's eyes as she looked at this man holding her daughter so sweetly. She swiped at the tears with her shaking fingers, and Ryder whispered to her, "Dakota wanted to watch cartoons and eat ice cream, so we all came down here to watch television with her. She climbed into JT's lap and fed him every other spoonful of ice cream and then fell asleep just before he did." He chuckled lightly. "We all went upstairs so we wouldn't wake them. Do you want to come up for a bit?"

Kayden watched JT's chest rise and fall a few times, his face more relaxed than she'd ever seen him. The firm set of his jaw was slackened, and in sleep he was more handsome than she ever dreamed he could be. No, wait, holding her daughter in his arms while she slept, that's what made him handsome. Definitely a keeper.

"Yeah, I can come up for a little while. I just hate to wake them up."

As they ascended the steps, she looked past the railing and watched both of them sleeping peacefully and she felt a little jealous.

34

J T slowly woke to the muffled sounds of people talking and laughing upstairs on the deck. He listened to see if he could tell who was still up chatting and bullshitting. The warm little bundle in his arms was breathing steadily and he felt peaceful and serene. Then he thought he heard the soft breathing of someone alongside him. He slowly opened his eyes to see the dark room was illuminated only from the glow of the clock above the bar and the outdoor lights in the windows. He turned toward the soft breathing and smiled when Kayden's sleeping form came into view in the chair next to his. Her left hand lay on Dakota's head, her right hand tucked under her cheek, her knees drawn up on the seat. He watched her sleep for a few moments, then he reached over and brushed her hand with his. Softly touching her fingers, he watched as her lashes fluttered then opened. She immediately smiled at him, then rubbed her eyes with the pads of her fingers, wiping the sleep away.

"You gave her ice cream," she whispered.

He furrowed his brows. "What makes you think that?"

She softly giggled and circled her fingers around her own lips. "Ice cream ring. Busted."

He chuckled. "You didn't say she couldn't have ice cream."

"You're right." She slowly sat up, turning in her chair to face him. "Did she have fun?"

He glanced down at the little angel, her blonde curls in disarray from her day. "Yeah. Everyone, including Mom and Dad, played hide and seek with her. She got a nickel for every person she found." He smiled as he remembered her giggles and squeals. "She can go to college on the money she made. The girl's a master at finding people."

Kayden laughed softly then quickly frowned.

"Hey. What just happened there?"

She looked at JT and softly said, "I don't play with her enough. I feel guilty."

He leaned over the chair as much as he could and reached across to her nape and pulled her close. "Never feel guilty. You're raising a wonderful little girl here. You're doing everything you can for her."

She leaned forward, and needing the contact with her, he kissed her lips. He reveled in the feel of her lips softly gliding over his and he never wanted this feeling to end.

When they pulled away, he whispered, "How's Duncan?"

"He had surgery again tonight to repair a nicked vein that had been missed during the first surgery. They say his chances are good. He was shot in the lung; the bullet hit a rib too. And, of course the vein. He'll be there for a while."

JT held her hand and the warmth from her touch felt like a wool blanket on a cold day. "I'm glad he'll be okay. Do they know what happened?"

Kayden stretched her back and rolled her shoulders. "Yeah. The growers came back to protect their crops and shot anyone getting too close. Another ranger was killed and two police officers were wounded as well. It's going to get rough around here."

JT looked at the clock on the wall and saw that it was just past midnight. "What time did you get here?"

"A little before ten. You two were already out." She sat back into the chair and looked over into his eyes.

❧

T aking a deep breath, she whispered, "I fell in love with you tonight, JT. Watching you hold my little girl and take care of her. I already had feelings for you, but it hit me when I looked at the two of you." She watched his face, which held a look of surprise, but softly, she repeated, "I fell in love with you."

He leaned forward and moved to the edge of his chair. Slowly standing, he carried Dakota to the bedroom he was using during his time here. She followed, watching him lay Dakota on the bed and gently cover her with a blanket. He turned and wrapped her tightly in his arms. His heartbeat was rapid and strong against her breasts. When he spoke to her, he sounded like he was trying to control himself—strained and tight. "I fell in love with you today, too, Kayden." His mouth captured hers in a searing kiss that left them both breathless. When they needed to breathe again, he glanced back at Dakota, then motioned toward the door. Taking her hand in his, he led her to the chair he'd just vacated, sat down and pulled her onto his lap. Pulling her tightly to him, he nestled her head on his shoulder and wrapped both arms tightly around her. "This won't be all that comfortable, but I want to sleep with you tonight, and I want to hear you tell me you love me again before I fall asleep."

He heard her sigh and nestle in before saying, "I love you, JT."

35

The morning sun streamed in through the window, slanting its warm rays across JT and Kayden. She opened her eyes slowly and sighed. His aftershave was forever imprinted on her mind. She'd never smell anyone that elicited the excitement and passion she felt when she smelled JT.

She lightly rubbed her face and eyes, waking her skin up for the day ahead. JT opened his eyes and a slow, sexy smile creased his handsome face. The beard he'd been growing the past few days—though not very long—looked thick and silky. He'd shaved it into a Vandyke the past day or two and the shape was very intriguing on him.

His hand came up to her face, lightly turning her to look at him. No hardship there. Then he pulled her down and kissed her lightly on the lips. Kayden deepened the kiss, enjoying kissing him first thing in the morning. The sound of a giggle caused them to stop and turn toward the sound.

"You guys are kissing." Dakota stood alongside the chair, hair a tangled mess, her clothing wrinkled and disheveled, but the biggest smile she could make graced her tiny face.

Kayden quickly sat up straight and moved to get up, but JT held her in place. He glanced at Dakota. "Want to join us in the chair?"

She nodded and quickly scrambled onto Kayden's lap and squirmed her way onto JT's other side. She looked at Kayden and giggled. "I made a lot of money last night and JT said I was good at finding people and I had ice cream and we watched cartoons."

Kayden chuckled. "What was your favorite part?"

Dakota pursed her lips. "Watching TV and eating ice cream with everyone. We had this whole room full and everyone was good. Nobody spilled and they let me watch what I wanted."

Touching the little wayward blonde curls, she smiled at her daughter. "That was very nice of them. Did you say thank you?"

Dakota looked down and a frown marred her precious little face. Tilting her chin up to look into her eyes, Kayden said, "Don't be sad. What's wrong?"

"I fell asleep and didn't say thank you." Her forlorn voice tore at Kayden's heart.

JT tsked and then said, "That's okay. Everyone is still here and when we have breakfast, you can tell them then."

That seemed to brighten her smile and she sat quietly with them for a few moments before repeating, "You guys were kissing." Then she giggled again.

"Yes, we were kissing. I like kissing JT. Does that bother you?"

Dakota's little face tilted up to look at JT, then back to her. "Nope. I like JT, too."

JT ruffled his fingers through her hair and kissed the top of her head. "I like you, too, Kota."

Footsteps above them signaled the family was waking. Chairs scooted across the floor and Dog grumbled something and then the word coffee. JT chuckled and looked at her. "Would you two like to freshen up in the bathroom and then we can go up and have some breakfast?"

"Yes. Thank you." She scooted off his lap and turned to pull Dakota from the little nest she'd made against JT. "Come on, baby. Let's go wash up."

~

JT stood and stretched. Sleeping in a chair, even a comfy one, wasn't nearly as restful as sleeping in a bed. He took the steps upstairs, wanting to have a conversation with his dad about Oakes driving down the road and what Dakota had told him. He reached the top step which landed in the kitchen and the aroma of fresh coffee made his mouth water. His mom was at the counter pulling eggs and bowls from their resting places to make breakfast; his dad was sitting at the kitchen table watching her. Actually, he was looking at her ass. JT chuckled—some things never changed.

"Morning." JT rubbed his stomach and stopped at the coffeepot, pouring three cups and delivering them to his parents before sitting down.

"Morning. Are Kayden and Dakota up?" Joci asked.

"Yeah. They're washing up. They'll be up here soon."

"Thanks. Morning." His dad eyed him briefly and then eagerly grabbed his coffee and inhaled deeply before sipping at his cup. "Mmm."

Catching his dad's gaze, he said, "You have a minute to talk about something?"

Leaning back in his chair, his dad nodded. "Yep."

JT quickly and quietly told him what he'd learned last night. "You can't tell Oakes what or how you know. I don't want Dakota to get in trouble."

"I wouldn't get her in trouble."

Little steps climbing toward them halted their conversation.

Breakfast was made and they gathered around the table to eat the pancakes his mom had made. Chatter and teasing went back and forth. Emma looked at JT and Kayden and with a sly smile on her face, she asked, "Did you all sleep well?"

Dakota nodded and said, "My mom and JT are getting married."

The room grew silent and all eyes turned toward them. Kayden leaned down. "Kota, you're not supposed to fib. Remember?"

Dakota turned to her, brows furrowed. "I'm not fibbing. You were kissing. Grandpa said you aren't supposed to kiss a boy unless you're getting married."

A few smirks graced faces, a couple of chuckles were heard, but Dakota continued on, "Actually, Grandpa says it like this." She wagged her little forefinger in front of her. "'Kota, you never kiss a boy till you know you're gonna get married to him. No good comes from kissing. Got it?'"

JT watched Kayden stifle a laugh and glance at him and then quickly away, a pretty pink staining her cheeks and neck. Looking down at Dakota, she said, "Well, Grandpa means you." She pointed to Dakota and then back to herself. "Not me. And JT and I are not getting married. Okay?"

Dakota's cute little face frowned. "Okay," she said quietly.

JT glanced at his brothers and saw them chuckling. He knew he'd be getting ribbed about this one later.

Chase and Frog came in the front door and bid good morning, then Frog said, "Dog, Chase's bike seems to be leaking a bit of oil. Just checking what time we're leaving this morning so we know if we have enough time to work on it before we go."

Jeremiah replied, "Around ten or so. Need help?"

"Naw. We got it," Chase answered.

"Come on in and eat, boys. Pancakes today," Joci offered.

Dakota giggled and looked at Jeremiah. "He called you Dog."

Leaning forward, he said, "That's my nickname. Just like your momma calls you Kota sometimes."

She cocked her little head. "Kota's part of my name. Dog's not part of yours."

Chuckles rounded the table and Dakota said, "What do I call you?"

Gunnar took that moment to speak up. He looked at Emma, then at his mom and dad. "You could call him Grandpa. That's what we'll be calling him in seven months."

Other than the audible gasps that were heard around the table, silence soon fell as the news was processed in the early morning hours. Joci jumped up from her chair and scooted around the table. She hugged Gunnar tightly. "Are you sure?"

The smile on Gunnar's face was brilliant. He reached for Emma and looking into her eyes, he said, "We're sure. We've known for about a week, but wanted everyone to be together when we announced it."

Congratulations and hugs were offered, making for an extremely light and happy mood.

Emma said, "We're going to move the wedding up so I'm not huge when we get married."

Jeremiah, still standing after hearing the news, leaned against the buffet along the wall and offered a compromise. "Have a double wedding." He glanced between Ryder and Gunnar.

Molly took Emma's hand in hers, and said, "That could be so much fun."

"Are you sure, Molly? You've been planning your own wedding with Ryder. Adding us to the mix might be a pain."

"No, it wouldn't. You'll have a hard time finding a venue, and we have one. Most of the same people will be there, except some of your friends, so a few more won't matter."

Emma turned to Gunnar. "What do you think?"

Gunnar kissed her lightly, then said to the group, "Let's talk about it a bit later. Okay?"

Emma nodded, the smile on her face brilliant. She glanced at Kayden and JT. "Gunnar was making me virgin Peach Bellini's the other night. We weren't ready to share the news yet."

Kayden smiled at her. "Oh, I hadn't even thought about that. Congratulations." She giggled and the sound zinged right through JT's body.

JT swallowed a lump in his throat, but smiled and congratulated his brother. He was happy for them, of course. Being an uncle was something he'd never thought about before, but now he was going to have a niece or nephew, and it made him a little melancholy for some reason. Taking a deep breath, he glanced at Kayden and caught her gaze with his. She smiled at him and his stomach flipped. The woman simply revved his engine.

"But I still don't know what I should call him," Dakota said, a little confusion in her voice.

Chuckles were heard as some of the group stood and cleared their plates.

JT leaned down to Dakota's ear, and said, "You can call him Dog. Or Jeremiah. Or Grandpa, if you like. That will help him get used to hearing it."

Dakota pursed her lips, thought for a moment, then said, "Okay. I'll think about it."

36

Kayden followed the women into the kitchen with a stack of dirty dishes. Many hands made for light work, her dad would say. Dakota followed JT around the dining room as he pushed in the chairs and straightened the table runner. She could hear Dakota chattering and asking him questions and he very patiently answered her.

Joci turned and said to her, "JT has another admirer, I see."

Kayden giggled. "Apparently."

"What are you going to do with Dakota today while you go to Sturgis?"

"I don't know. I thought I'd call my dad and see how he's feeling. He loves having her around and as long as he's recovered, I can go, but I can cut the day short if he's afraid he'll get tired."

Emma offered up. "If it wasn't for the Build-Off, I'd stay home with her, but I just hate to miss seeing JT's big day."

"Aww. I appreciate the offer, but my dad has had Dakota around since she was born. They get on well together."

With the dishes washed and put away, Kayden went in search of JT and Dakota. The downstairs of the house was empty, but she could hear the guys outside talking. She opened the door to see a line of bikes in the driveway, and buckets of soapy water here and there. She scanned the group and easily found JT and Dakota washing his bike. She had suds up to her elbows and her little purple shirt was wet, but the smile on her face as she rubbed a soapy sponge on JT's fender was priceless.

She maneuvered her way around the obstacles and stood just off the side, watching him explain how he washed his motor and the frame of the bike. Dakota squatted down just like he did as he pointed to different parts and named them.

She pulled her phone from her pocket and snapped pictures of them together. The clicking caught their attention. "Mommy, JT showed me the pimary."

Kayden chuckled. "Primary case."

"Yeah."

Laughing, she said, "That's something good to know. Now, I'm afraid we need to say goodbye and go see Grandpa."

"Do we have to go? I'm not finished yet," she whined.

JT gently took the sponge from her hand and turned Dakota to face him. "Hey there, I'll see you later on, okay?"

Dakota hesitated before finally responding. "Okay."

JT stood and wrapped his arms around Kayden. Gruffly, he said, "I'll see you later, too. Do you need a ride into Sturgis?"

She shook her head. "No. I'm fine, but yes, I'll see you later. I'll be there for you today. When they announce the winner of the Build-Off."

He kissed her briefly. "Thank you."

Setting up her table in Sturgis, Kayden mulled over the events of the past few days. Her life had changed in so many ways. She was in love with a wonderful man who was part of a wonderful family. She'd decided to have the conversation with her father about selling the bar, leaving her free to pursue her Kayden's Concealed Carry clothing lines. She had a licensing deal in the works for KCC, though she had to finalize the plans tomorrow. Life was finally looking up, that's for sure.

"Well, looky here. Kayden's trying to sell clothing for women to protect themselves." The sarcasm, stench, and the voice alerted her to the fact that Boon had found her here in Sturgis.

"Go away, Boon," she responded while continuing to set out the thigh holsters on the rack her dad made just for them.

He picked up a couple of the expertly arranged corsets laying on the table and whistled.

"Bet you look right sexy in this. You got one on now?" He reached forward to lift her shirt but she stepped back and slapped at his hand.

"Get the fuck out of here right now, Boon. And don't touch my things unless you're buying."

The sickening laugh that he emitted made her stomach roll.

"For your information, I have every right to be here," he baited.

She refolded the corsets he'd disrupted and rearranged them. When he touched them again, she slapped his hands, and then shoved him away from the table.

"I believe she asked you to leave. You may have a right to be here in Sturgis, but you don't have the right to harass anyone."

Kayden watched JT's jaw tense and relax as he stared Boon down.

"Don't have all your back up with you today, pretty boy." Boon sarcastically glanced around.

"They're here. Waiting," he slowly threatened.

Boon chuckled and Kayden swallowed the lump forming in her throat. This could go so wrong.

A police officer walked up to them. "I believe we told you Devils any more trouble this week and you'll finish the rally in jail."

Boon looked at the tips of his boots and snickered. "Not in any trouble, officer. Just don't like being threatened."

The officer looked at JT. "Have you threatened him, sir?"

JT looked the officer square in the eye and shook his head no. "Not at all. The lady asked him to leave and not touch her merchandise unless he was buying and he chose to ignore her."

The officer turned to Boon. "You have anything to say to that?"

Boon glanced at Kayden and JT. In an exaggerated bow, he said to Kayden, "I'll be seeing you around, *Miss*." He nodded at JT and menacingly said, "Both of you."

He nodded to the officer and then strode away.

"If everything is all right, I'll leave you two be. We'll be watching the area for the Devils, and I'm scheduled to be on this block all evening."

JT held out his hand and shook the officer's. "Thank you."

He leaned across the table to Kayden, pulled her to him with his fingers around the nape of her neck and kissed her lips. "You okay?"

Letting out a shaky breath, she replied, "Yeah. Thank you." Running her fingers across his cheek, she whispered, "How did you know he was back here?"

Pulling back and sliding his fingers in his pockets he glanced around. "I saw him and a couple of his minions walking through the Build-Off room. Rumor has it that the owner of the red bike in the Build-Off against me is a cousin to Boon. They were threatening voters and trying to stack the deck. The judges kicked them out. Idiots are wearing their colors, so it isn't hard to spot them."

She let out a deep breath. "Those assholes have their gross hands in everything around here. Can't even have an honest bike contest without them trying to slant the votes." She glanced in the direction Boon had walked and scrunched up her face.

JT kissed her lightly again and backed away. "Gotta get back. Call me if you need me."

She watched his sexy backside walk into the other half of the building. His back straight and proud, his hair tamed into his customary ponytail, his shoulders broad and strong. She was a lucky girl, all right. She felt even more fortunate when she saw a few women glance his way as he strode through the building. Yep. Lucky.

37

J T sauntered back into the Build-Off section of the building. The heat was rising as it filled with people. This was the day they all turned out for the unveiling of the new winner for the year. Not only was first prize major bragging rights, but a check for fifty thousand dollars, the cover of *Steelhorse* magazine, and a big ass trophy to display in his or her shop. If his dad wouldn't let him design and build at Rolling Thunder, JT would use the money to start his own business. If he won, that is. The way the Devils were trying to manipulate the votes, he'd be lucky to win now.

He approached the stage where each of the three bikes were on turntables, rotating so people could see the whole bike before they voted. Lights shown on the chrome and the metallic in his white paint glimmered as it slowly spun. She was a beauty. He looked at the other two bikes and tried to be very critical of his compared to theirs. They were so different, so it was hard to say one was a clear winner over another. And it's hard to be completely critical when you have a personal stake in one of the entries. He'd have to wait and see. That was the hard part.

His dad and brothers approached and nodded toward a corner

alongside the stage. "Let's go have a little chat." His dad's jaw was tight and his posture rigid, causing his stomach to turn a notch.

As they huddled together, his dad said, "We just overheard a disturbing conversation."

JT held up a hand. "If you mean about the Devils stacking the votes, I've heard."

Dog's brows furrowed. "Stacking the votes? For the Build-Off?"

"Yeah. Isn't that what you were going to say?"

"No." His dad looked at all the boys as he continued. "Three of the Devils were talking about 'the old bastard at the bar' and how they were going to get what he owed them. Said Rog's whore would have to make good on it if he didn't."

JT's back straightened and his jaw tensed. The roiling in his stomach caused him to put a hand over his abdomen and suck in a breath. "What do you think they meant by that? I mean, I know what I think it means, but what do you think?"

Ryder and Gunnar both looked at him; their faces said it all and it wasn't good.

His dad answered for them. "She's likely in a bit of danger. But, if Oakes is involved with these guys in some deal and she knows about it, she needs to fess up. If she's also involved, she needs protection."

JT clenched his jaw. "She's not involved in anything shady."

Jeremiah looked into his eyes. "JT, you need to be real. Oakes shot someone the other night in the bar. One of his guns was stolen and he knew about it but didn't say anything. Kayden found a cash box of money and just put it away as if she hadn't seen it. So many things don't add up."

He rubbed his forehead and rotated his neck—fucking tension just wouldn't ease up.

"Boon was just back there a while ago harassing her." JT let out a long breath. Keeping his worry in check was necessary. "She didn't look or sound like someone in cahoots with him."

Ryder cleared his throat. "I'm thinking we need to watch her a bit closer. Looks like you're in the perfect position to do that." He ended with a chuckle and JT scowled at him.

"You want me to spy on Kayden?" he asked incredulously.

Ryder shook his head. "Not spy, just stay close to see if you can get an idea of what's going on."

Gunnar added, "How about this? We know Oakes is involved in something that, at the least, is under the table. At most, we don't know. How about you ask Kayden straight out what she knows? Tell her what we overheard and gage her reaction."

JT took a deep breath. This trip was sucking ass. The only good thing about it was he had met Kayden, but even that silver lining was beginning to tarnish.

~

K ayden glanced around the room once again. She was beginning to feel paranoid. All day there were at least two Devils in the building, and each time she glanced in their direction, they were watching her. The little hairs at the back of her neck prickled and the unease in her gut grew to almost overwhelming.

She quickly packed away the remaining garments from her table and stored them in the locker provided to vendors. She tucked her earnings into the hidden pocket in the KCC belt she wore and smoothed down her loose fitting gray tank. She didn't want to miss the Build-Off finale. And she hoped beyond hope that the devils weren't rewarded for their bad deeds. They were becoming more and more powerful by the day.

She walked from the locker room through the vendor side of the building and entered the Build-Off room, constantly checking the location of the Devils who seemed overly interested in her. The noise was deafening and the temperature sweltering with all the warm bodies packed into it. This was the culmination of the rally. The races had ended today, and this evening the Build-Off finale followed by a band and more than likely drinking into the night. She'd be happy to skip that part of it. She loved listening to a good band, but she'd seen enough drunks in her life to last her into forever. Her father used to be a roaring drunk, back in the day before her mom died. She squirmed and squeezed her way through the hordes of people as her nose was assaulted by the over-cologned, sweaty bodies squeezed into the building.

Standing at the edge of the stage where JT would see her, she tried to ignore the uneasy feeling crawling through her stomach. Probably nerves. She was nervous for JT; that had to be it. His stomach must be so much worse. She looked over the crowd trying to see any of the Sheppards or their crew, but the faces blended together. She took another glance around, checking on the location of the Devils. The announcer walked out on stage and the roar from the crowd made her ears vibrate. She plugged her fingers into her ears for a bit of relief, her eyes transfixed on the stage to see JT walk out.

The announcer held his hand up and waited for the room to quiet before speaking. As the volume began to lower, he asked, "Everyone ready for the big finale?"

Even her chest vibrated with the rumble all the yelling caused. The announcer first did a shout-out to the event judges who were responsible for the first round of judging which is how these three bikes made it up on the stage. He asked them to raise their hands if they were in the audience and all heads turned to locate them. That's when Kayden's stomach did a serious flop. Boon stood next to one of the judges, but the scowl on his face was positively menacing.

She followed his line of sight and saw members of a rival gang—Aces of Antioch—taunting a few of the Devils. Things like this never turned out good.

The announcer continued by asking the builders to step out on stage. The three men walked out from backstage and again the eruption of the crowd was deafening. She screamed right along with them this time, and her heart fluttered as she took in JT. His black t-shirt stretched so tight across his broad chest, allowing the definition of his muscles and abs to be seen. He was so sexy. His jeans fit him to perfection as usual. The man was simply striking. While his ponytail suited him, she wanted his hair flowing free so she could dig her fingers in it while he rode her. Moisture sped to the juncture of her thighs at the thought. Damn.

He glanced in her direction and winked when he saw her and if she were lesser of a woman, she would have swooned. Seriously.

The announcer began, "All right, act like you've seen men before, ladies." Laughter. "Okay, third runner up will receive five hundred dollars, a small article in *Steelhorse* Magazine—the sponsor of this event—and a wall plaque. And that winner is..."

"Down and Dirty Bike Shop from the great state of Texas, builder Bradley Hammond." The bike Boon was trying to stack the votes for. Third place. At least they didn't accomplish what they'd set out to do.

JT and the other builder clapped and walked over to Bradley and shook hands. As JT turned to walk back to his position alongside his bike, shots rang out. The crowd scattered and pushing and shoving caused mayhem to reign. People were pushed to the floor, more fled to the doors, but a bottleneck was created as too many people tried to leave at the same time.

Another shot rent the air and another. Kayden was pushed against the stage, the air whooshing from her lungs. The next thing she knew she was hauled up onto the stage by strong hands under her arms and pulled behind the curtain. She tried to cry out but no sound would come. She heard shushing in her ear as JT's strong arms came around her from behind. He held her close while he gently lay them down on the floor.

"Breathe in deeply, and let it out slowly, Angel," he murmured into her ear.

The chaos out front was frightening. When she felt her breathing return, she nodded her head. She turned in his arms and wrapped her arms around his neck. She shook from head to toe and gripped him so hard she thought she could snap him in two.

He whispered, "Keep breathing, baby." He held her tight. After just a few moments, he pulled away. "You stay right here. I need to peek out and see if I can find my family."

"No. JT. Don't go. It's Boon. I saw him watching the Aces as they were fighting with a couple of his guys. If he sees you after earlier today, he just might shoot you, too."

"I'll stay behind the curtain, but I have to look."

She had his shirt in her fists as she held him next to her. "Please don't."

"Angel, I have to. Stay here. Stay down." He gently pried her fingers from his shirt and crawled to the edge of the curtain next to the wall. She watched his back as he tried to locate his family. Trying to hear anything useful, she listened as the chaos continued. Even if the noise hadn't been deafening, the raging beat of her heart would have drowned out everything anyway.

Peeking between the curtain and the wall, JT spotted his dad and Gunnar on the floor helping to stop the bleeding from a wound in a man's chest. Gunnar had the man's shirt wadded around the wound and was applying pressure while his dad was looking for other wounds. He noticed two men lying on the ground, face down, and men on top of them holding them down. One man was bucking and yelling and another man plowed his fist into the screaming man's face, effectively knocking him out. The other man seemed to have submitted to being held down, or they'd already knocked him out.

JT's heart pounded. This brought back too many tortured memories of Afghanistan. He'd never dreamed he'd feel that way here at home. The slickness on his palms and the trickle of sweat down his back had nothing to do with the heat this time. He turned and looked at Kayden. "I have to go and help them."

"No, JT; please don't go out there."

He crawled toward her. "Kayden, I have to. The shooting has stopped and it looks as though the men have been wrestled to the ground and are being detained by citizens. Stay here. If you don't want to stay here, come with me and I'll find my mom and the girls and you can be with them. I'd prefer that, by the way."

He watched her process this for a brief moment before she

scooted toward him. Making sure it was all clear, he checked from behind the curtain again and then slowly stepped out from his hiding place, not wanting to make any quick movements. His dad looked up and nodded to him. People were still trying to push their way out of the building. The noise had lessened, but still the yelling and screaming was all that could be heard.

He held Kayden's hand as they made their way down the five steps from the stage. "No sudden movements, just slow and steady. Okay?"

"Yeah."

Landing on the floor, he maneuvered them along the front of the stage and over to where his dad and Gunnar were. He knelt down. "Where's Mom and the girls?"

His dad nodded. "Over helping Ryder with another shooting victim. He was shot in the neck and head."

He glanced at the rest of his family, helping victims. Molly was calming a woman, must have been the wife or girlfriend of the victim Ryder was helping. She kept her arms wrapped tightly around the hysterical woman to keep her out of the way. Looking down at Kayden, she said, "I'll help you with whatever you need."

Seeing a woman lying close holding her arm tightly to her stomach, JT and Kayden stepped around debris to help her. "Where are you injured?" he asked

Through tears she said, "My arm was broken when I was pushed to the ground."

He removed her fingers from her injured arm when police stormed in all doors at once. "Police. Everyone freeze. Hands on your heads. Lace your fingers."

Slowly, they laced their fingers on their heads as the police stood at each exit and waited for everyone to comply. Looking at the woman JT was just beginning to help, an officer ordered, "Hands on your head and lace your fingers. Now!"

She began crying and JT addressed the officer. "Her arm is broken."

The officer eyed the woman and said, "Put your good arm up on your head until we have assessed this room. Please."

Several officers stood guard watching the people in the room while three officers slowly made their way to the victims. Jeremiah addressed one of the officers, nodding to the two shooters. "Those are your shooters under the knees of those men over there. They tackled them to the ground after the shots began." Looking down at the man he was helping, he said, "This man has a gunshot wound to the chest. That man over there..." he said, nodding to Ryder and the women, "has a gunshot wound to the neck and head."

"Who are you?" the officer asked.

"Jeremiah Sheppard. Former Marine Corps."

The officer nodded. "Are you triage trained?"

"Not formally. Just what we learned in battle." He nodded to JT and Ryder. "Those are my sons and also Marine Corps battle trained."

The officer asked for Jeremiah's ID, which he slowly pulled from his pocket. Once he was cleared, the officer asked him to continue to help the man until paramedics could arrive. Making his way to Ryder and then JT, he asked them each for their IDs and once they were cleared, they continued to help their respective victims. A couple of nurses had been in the crowd and also were tending to the injured.

Paramedics arrived and loaded the victims into ambulances; the police carted away the two shooters. One was Boon; the other was one of the Aces.

38

It was after seven o'clock when they were able to leave the scene of the Build-Off shooting. No one had officially won the trophy for this year, but they'd know more in the next few days how the winner would be notified. Though it would be anticlimactic, after the events of today, anticlimactic sounded damn good.

Kayden offered to bring the women home in her Jeep. They were all shook up after the shooting and being able to sit in the Jeep on the hour long ride helped them relax. JT eagerly looked forward to riding and letting the road take away the horrors of today. Riding with his family was one of his greatest pleasures. The bikes easily weaved through traffic, and he'd lost sight of the Jeep long ago.

As the wind whipped his hair and he rode the curves of the road, he felt himself relax just a bit. Finally pulling into the parking lot of OK's, he continued through the parking lot and to the garage below Kayden's apartment. He shut his bike off and dismounted. Pulling the hair band from his hair, he massaged his scalp and fingered the snarls as he slowly walked toward the bar. Soft crying caught his attention and he stopped and listened to see what direction it was coming from.

He walked toward the crying, which seemed to be coming from

Oakes' old garage behind Kayden's. Stepping as quietly as he could on the gravel, he trained his ears on the sound. It sounded like a little girl. His heart began pounding in his chest and he called out, "Dakota?"

The crying stopped, but he called again. "Dakota? It's JT, are you okay?"

The service door was cracked open and he stepped inside the darkened garage. Feeling the wall for a light switch, he couldn't find one. He pulled his phone from his pocket, turned on the flashlight app, and slowly canted the light around the room.

"Dakota? Honey, it's JT. Come out so I can help you."

Softly, a little voice sniffled, "JT? I need help."

His heart sped and the lump in his throat threatened to suffocate him. Swallowing several times, he asked, "Honey, where are you?"

"In the back room."

Roving the light over the contents of the garage, he saw Oakes' motorhome covered in a thick layer of dust. His pickup truck sat next to that and various rakes, shovels, and lawn equipment lined the walls. Continuing around the room, he saw the old wooden door on the wall that butted up to the hills behind the garage. JT made his way to that door and tried the knob. It turned, but the door seemed to be stuck.

"Dakota, are you in there?"

Crying, she managed, "Yes. I'm scared and Grandpa is hurt."

JT slipped his phone into his pocket and pulled on the door with both hands. He got it to budge a little but not enough. It seemed to be stuck on the bottom. Pulling his phone out once again, he trained his light at the bottom of the door and found an old differential from a truck had been pushed in front of it. Once again sliding his phone into his pocket, he tugged and pulled and was finally able to move the differential enough to open the door.

He turned the knob and opened the door. He knelt down and Dakota jumped into his arms, her wet little face buried into his neck as she cried. He shone his light into the makeshift room, cut into the hill behind the garage. It had the eerie appearance of a cave, but he could see it wasn't all that deep. Makeshift wooden shelves lined the walls and sitting on those shelves were a few bricks of what looked like marijuana.

He moved his light to the ground, and there laid Oakes—his face ashen—not moving. JT scooted to Oakes' side, Dakota hanging on to his neck with shaking arms. "What happened, Kota?"

"The men were here and they were mad at Grandpa. They yelled and yelled but he told them he'd meet them tomorrow with their shit. When they finally left, we came out here. Grandpa told me to stay close to him and not wander. But when we got out here, those bad men came back. They fought with Grandpa and I hid right there." She pointed to the ground under a shelf where she must have tucked herself.

"They took some of Grandpa's shit." She pointed to the shelves and the remaining blocks.

JT hugged her close. "Probably shouldn't say that word anymore, Kota," he said softly.

She whimpered. "Okay."

"Then what happened?"

"Grandpa put his hands on his chest and then fell down. Those bad men left and I couldn't get Grandpa to wake up. I couldn't get out of here. So, I cried."

JT held her close as he pulled his phone up and tapped his dad's icon. As he waited for his father to answer, he whispered to Dakota, "It's okay, honey. I'm here now."

"JT, where are you?"

"Dad, I'm in the back behind Kayden's garage. Oakes has another garage back here and he's in here with Dakota. You better come quickly and call an ambulance."

JT ended the call and felt Oakes for a heartbeat. Finding a very faint heartbeat, he let out a long breath. He told Dakota, "It's going to be okay, honey. We'll get Grandpa help."

Dog, Ryder, Gunnar, Chase, and Frog came blasting through the garage door yelling for JT.

"We're back here, head toward the hillside of the garage. You're going to need your flashlights; I don't think there's lights in this garage."

Almost immediately, one phone after another began lighting up the place. As they made their way toward JT and Dakota, he said, "I think Oakes had another heart attack, based on what Dakota just told me."

Dakota began crying softly, and JT continued to hold her close to his chest and whisper in her ear that all would be all right.

For the second time in a day, the Sheppards dealt with police and paramedics. Oakes was loaded into the ambulance as Kayden and the women pulled into the parking lot. Kayden ran toward the ambulance and JT, still holding Dakota, intercepted her path. Kayden's panicked look disappeared when she saw that Dakota was all right. She held her arms out and Dakota happily hugged her momma. "Oakes had a heart attack, Kayd," JT softly informed her. "He's still alive, but it isn't good."

Her eyes filled with tears, but he continued, "The police want to talk to you." He took a deep breath. "Your dad had a large amount of marijuana in that garage and they think he's been selling." He watched her face as the surprise flitted over it.

She looked at the ambulance and then back to JT. "What? He'd never do that. Why do they think that?"

"Kayd, the Devils came here and fought with him." He nodded at Dakota who still had her head down on Kayden's shoulder, her little face in the crook of her neck. "She heard it and saw it. She saw them steal bricks from your dad's garage."

The tears slipped down her cheeks, but not a sound came from her. She watched the ambulance pull out of the parking lot, lights flashing, sirens whining. His heart broke for her.

"Ma'am, we'd like to have a word with you." Kayden turned toward the police officer and nodded her head. JT held his arms out for Dakota and she snuggled back into his chest where she'd been before. "I'll take her upstairs and get her ready for bed." Kayden nodded as she followed the officer to his car. JT caught his mom's attention and motioned her toward them.

"I'm going to need some assistance in getting Dakota ready for bed. She needs a bath and I've never done that before. Will you help me?"

"Of course, honey." She patted Dakota's little back and they walked toward the apartment. JT glanced back once and saw Kayden standing next to the officer's car, her arms wrapped around her middle, hugging herself, her face wet with tears. He couldn't remember a time he'd felt lower.

K ayden shoved her hands into her hair and held them there. She felt numb. First the shooting, now this. As she thought back on certain events in her life, it made sense now. About the time she got pregnant with Dakota, things changed around here. She'd been so wrapped up in herself that she either didn't notice or chose not to think about it. The Devils came around a bit more and she assumed it was because Rog was friends with some of them. Then her dad caught Rog stealing from the till and fired him. That's when things started getting nasty. Rog went to jail for robbing a store in Deadwood and things settled for a while. New customers were coming into the bar and she thought things were going good. The big house came on the market and Kayden brought the idea to her dad about the vacation rental to earn more money. He had the money for her in no time, said he had it in his savings. Then they had money for remodeling. Two years ago when she needed money for an attorney to begin the process of termination of Rog's parental rights, he helped her out. But that's when things got nasty with the Devils. They started coming around and chasing away their customers, and her dad told her it was because of the mica. They still had some regular customers, but that was about it. Now she wondered if something else transpired between him and the Devils. She hated to think about it, but the police told her they thought Oakes had stolen from them. They'd been watching the bar for a little while now and suspected something was going down at the bar.

The regular customers were not actually customers at all, but buyers.

She slowly made her way up the stairs to her apartment. This was a day she'd never forget and one she'd very much like to. She'd called the hospital and was told her father was resting and that visitors were discouraged until tomorrow. Fine by her. She was pissed and tired and not in the mood to go and have to rein in her anger at him tonight.

Opening the door to her apartment, she heard JT's low sexy voice softly reading a book to Dakota. Peering into the living room, he sat in her recliner. Dakota rested in the crook of his arm, her eyes droopy, but she looked peaceful. She was wearing her pink nightgown and her little bare feet rested on his thigh. If you can fall in love twice with the same person in the same week, she just did. He looked up at her and a slow sexy smile turned his face from soft and endearing to dangerously sexy in a nanosecond.

Dakota peered around her book and sleepily said, "Hi, Mommy."

"Hi, baby. Looks like you and JT have things handled in here."

"Yeah. And Joci helped me take a bath."

JT grinned. "I've never done that and Mom said she'd help, so I took advantage."

"Are you almost finished?"

Dakota yawned. "Yeah." She rubbed her little eyes. "Is Grandpa okay?"

Kayden glanced at JT, then back to Dakota. "Yeah. He's resting now."

JT set the book on the table beside the chair and stood holding Dakota in his arms. "Let's get you to bed, little one."

Kayden started down the hall before them, and he followed, carrying her precious bundle. She pulled the comforter back and JT laid Dakota in her bed, kissed her forehead, and said, "See you in the morning, Kota."

In her sleep-filled voice she said, "Okay. Thank you for saving me."

Kayden furrowed her brows. She hadn't heard this part of the story yet. JT stood and Kayden swooped in to kiss Dakota good night. "Sleep tight. I'll love you always, Dakota."

"I'll love you always, Momma. You too, JT."

He instantly put his hand over his heart and Kayden thought it was the sweetest thing she'd ever seen. Definitely a keeper.

His voice low and soft, he said, "I'll love you always, too, Dakota."

She smiled and nestled herself into her pillow and closed her eyes.

39

Kayden looked at JT as they entered the kitchen. "Beer?"

"Yes. God, what a day."

She pulled two beers from the refrigerator and popped the tops off with the opener she pulled from the drawer. Handing one to him, they tapped their bottles together and both of them had a nice long drink. He took her hand and walked to the living room and sat on the sofa, pulling her down next to him.

"You okay?"

She sighed heavily. "I'm okay, I think." Her fingers absently picked at the label on the beer bottle where she pulled and tugged until the whole label came off. "I don't know what to think. I didn't know he was dealing. I feel so stupid that it was going on right under my nose, and I didn't know a damn thing."

"That's how they do it. You can't let too many people in on what you're doing. More risk of word getting out that way. Plus, I suspect he never wanted you to know."

"Yeah. Tell me about saving Dakota."

JT explained everything to her and she sat stoically and listened, anger bubbling up in her chest so powerful she wanted to scream.

Right in front of her little girl, his little granddaughter, he messed with them and that shit. Pissed her off.

"I don't know what to do, JT. I'm so mad at him, I want to hit him full force. How could he do this? He's always been so good. All these years since he's been sober, I thought we walked the narrow line. And he put Kota and me in danger."

JT sat quietly for a few moments. Finally, he said, "I know what you mean. I'm pissed at him for all of this, too. He's not the man I thought I knew. And the fact that he put the two women I love in danger, well that rankles something awful." He wrapped his arm around her shoulders, kissed her lips and laid his head on top of hers. "But, in truth, he might not make it through this heart attack, Kayd. You need to make peace with that. And don't let him die with you angry at him; that will haunt you."

She sniffled as the tears sprang to her eyes. He was right. Again. He was always right. She sat enjoying the warmth and comfort of his arms, the smell of his aftershave, and the fact that he loved her and her daughter and they loved him just made it so much better. She'd be okay. They'd be okay.

After a long silence, he said, "You'll probably lose the big house, you know. He bought it with drug money, so the feds will take it."

"Yeah. The police mentioned as much."

"The bar was purchased long before this, so you can sell it. You and Dakota can come back to Wisconsin and live with me."

She looked up into his eyes. "I can't live in sin with an impressionable little girl in the house."

"Is that still a thing? Living in sin?"

She giggled. "Probably not."

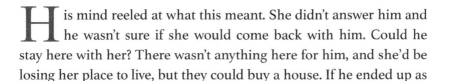

His mind reeled at what this meant. She didn't answer him and he wasn't sure if she would come back with him. Could he stay here with her? There wasn't anything here for him, and she'd be losing her place to live, but they could buy a house. If he ended up as the winner of the Build-Off, he'd have fifty thousand dollars to use as seed money.

He sat staring at the picture on the wall across from the sofa. It looked like an older picture of this place before this apartment had been completed. She turned into him and kissed his lips. Softly at first but her lips became more insistent, her body pushing into his. She felt perfect against him. Her soft body molded itself to his. His hands sought her ass and pulled her onto his lap. Yep, she was a balm for his wounds. He hoped like hell he was her balm.

She pulled back and looked deep into his eyes. "We should take this into the bedroom. Dakota sleeps soundly, but it's been a traumatic day for her, and just in case she wakes, she shouldn't see what I want to do to you."

Ah, that sounded promising, indeed. His voice came out raspy when he said, "Lead the way, baby."

She stood and pulled him from the sofa. She walked to the door to check the locks, then to the other end of the apartment and her bedroom. He breathed deeply upon entering her domain; it smelled like her and he wanted to be immersed in her fully, inside and out. She turned and the look she gave him practically had his cock jumping out of his jeans. Painfully hard from just a look, as soon as she touched him, he'd be beyond the point of no return.

He closed the door quietly behind them and flicked the lock, just in case. She dropped to her knees and the blood rushed out of his head. Slowly unzipping his jeans, she licked her lips and he couldn't take his eyes from her little pink tongue and the glistening trail it left behind. She flicked her gaze up to him and smirked. His face said it all.

Pulling his jeans from his hips, she tugged his briefs, making sure to relieve his cock first from its confines. She hummed appreciatively. "You're a magnificent specimen, JT."

That teasing wet tongue licked him from balls to top and precum instantly oozed from the tip of his cock. She hummed as her mouth completely encased him and the vibration sent lightning flashing through his body. He thought his head would explode. She sucked and licked him a few times, then held him in her hand, pumping him smoothly while she dipped her head and licked his balls. The groan he emitted came from deep within his core, a sound he'd never heard from himself before. He felt her smile against his balls and she gently pushed on his legs to spread them wider. Dipping her head further under him and turning herself so she was sitting, she licked his ass from the puckered opening to his balls. "Fuck me," he whispered.

She giggled. "Oh, I am definitely going to fuck you, baby."

His knees began to shake; he'd never before felt the sensations flying through his body. His head filled with visions of her, and only her, in every conceivable position. She quickly pulled her t-shirt off and slid her little shorts from her body. In two quick smooth movements, her bra and panties were on the floor, and her sexy, naked body was a feast for his hungry eyes.

He reached down and took her hand in his and pulled her to her feet. "I'm going to fall flat on my face if you don't let me lie down."

Her seductive full lips, still moist from her ministrations on him, called to him in the most profound way.

She took two steps toward the bed and turned to pull him down on it. He laid back with his feet still on the floor and she climbed up his body, kissing him and licking him as she moved. Reaching his lips, she plunged her tongue into his mouth and he held her head in his hands and consumed her lips. His tongue tasted every surface of her mouth, his lips slid smoothly over hers. She pulled back and whispered, "Let's cowboy up, big guy."

As he processed what she'd said, she turned her body, straddling him, her ass pointing toward his face. Gorgeous. She took his cock in her hands and pumped him as she palmed his balls, gently running her fingers over the coarse hairs. She tossed her head back, then looked over her shoulder, the knowing smile on her face, she was trying to drive him mad with desire, and she was doing a fabulous job of it. She lifted herself slightly, placed his hard cock at her opening and slowly slid down. She moaned as she fully seated on him.

His hands palmed her firm ass, loving the way his fingers left little imprints after he squeezed. She leaned forward, and placing her hands on his knees, she looked back and asked, "Ready?"

"Do it to me. Fuck me, Angel."

She pumped his cock in the most erotic way. Her ass bouncing, the skin lightly rippling each time she landed firmly on his groin, then lifting again. The sight before him was one he'd remember when he was in his eighties and beyond, should he live that long. Her dark hair swayed on her back, and when he looked down and could watch his cock disappear into her body, he had to fight not to lose his cool. Damn.

He wet his finger in his mouth and slowly slid it into her puckered hole. She slowed her milking of his cock and dropped her head down, moaning, and he gently pushed his finger into her. Her warmth sucked him in. As he pulled his finger out and then back in, he could feel her pussy pulse around his cock.

"Damn it, Kayd, this is the most erotic feeling in the world. This vision I have of you is simply perfection."

She whispered, "JT."

She began pumping him again, faster this time, moving her body so sensuously it was like a perfectly choreographed dance. He continued to watch her ass and then his cock disappear inside of her. His balls drew up into his body and he ground out, "Kayd. Get there."

Her voice was husky and low. "Yes." She pulsed and moaned as her orgasm hit and even though she'd stopped pumping him as her orgasm flowed through her, he came watching and listening to her. Fucking fantastic.

40

Kayden felt JT slip from the bed as quiet as a mouse and steal into the bathroom. She heard the shower turn on and rolled over and hugged his pillow, deeply breathing in his scent. He'd woken in the middle of the night a few times and always pulled her into his arms. He'd kiss her head and whisper, "I love you," before drifting back to sleep. Her heart was full.

She couldn't go to Wisconsin with him though—not while her dad was here, anyway. She didn't know what would happen to him; it was a real possibility that he would go to jail. Now they'd have legal expenses and who knew how long all of that would take. Trials could be long and drawn out and it would involve the Devils, something she was loathe to even give thought to. Today she had to keep her temper in check when she spoke to her dad. And she hoped to God he wasn't responsible for shooting Duncan. She'd never be able to face Payton again if that were the case. Luckily, Duncan was going to survive, but still.

She rose from the bed and pulled on her little gray jersey robe. She padded to the kitchen and started a pot of coffee. The open concept allowed her to stand in the kitchen and look into the living room. She glanced out of the living room window at her father's garage and her stomach plummeted at what had happened to her little girl in that shed. While in time she'd forget about it, Dakota had spent around an hour and a half in there, scared out of her mind, Oakes lying there, unable to help her. Thank God JT heard her crying.

The bathroom door opened and JT stepped into her line of sight. Showered and fresh, he looked and smelled like a fresh new day. The blue t-shirt he had on looked scrumptious on him, of course; everything did. He stepped behind her and slipped his arms around her waist. She leaned her head back against his chest and he kissed her temple. "Staring at it doesn't change anything."

She turned into his arms. "I know. It just makes me sad when I think of what Dakota had to go through. I'm so grateful to you for saving her and Dad." Tears threatened and she quickly changed her thought direction to stop them from flowing.

"Hey. She's safe. You're safe. That's all that matters, Kayd."

"Yeah." Wiping at her eyes, she added, "Coffee?"

"Yeah. Today promises to be another full day."

"God, already this morning I'm tired at the thought of everything we have to do."

She pulled two cups from the cupboard and filled them with the freshly brewed coffee, the aroma swirling around the room. She added creamer to both of their cups and turned to hand JT his coffee.

"I didn't tell you something about your dad last night. The other day when I brought Dakota home to the house while you visited Payton and Duncan, we saw your dad drive past the house and turn into the hills. Dakota told me he goes there a lot and comes out with packages. He makes her sit in the truck while he goes in there. I think he must have another little cave dug up there where he's hiding more drugs. If the cops didn't go up there last night, they'll be crawling all around the place today."

Kayden rubbed her forehead with her fingers. "God, it just doesn't stop."

He kissed her temple and walked them into the living room to sit on the sofa. Dakota woke up and tiptoed out to see what was going on. She giggled and ran to JT when she spied him. He quickly set his cup on the table between the sofa and recliner and caught her in his arms. Settling her on his lap, he asked, "Did you sleep good last night?"

"Yep. I dreamed I was a princess and I was saved by the prince."

He chuckled. "You don't need to wait for a prince to save you, Kota. You're a smart girl, you can save the prince instead."

She furrowed her little brows and looked up at JT. "I can?"

"Yes. You can. Always remember that."

"Okay." Her sweet little face turned up to Kayden. "Are we going to see Grandpa today?"

"Yes. We're going right after breakfast. Are you hungry?"

Before answering, she turned to JT. "Are you having breakfast with us?"

"Yes. Is that okay?"

"Mmhmm." She nodded her head vigorously.

Kayden giggled. "Okay. Give me a hug and a kiss and go get dressed and I'll make us something to eat."

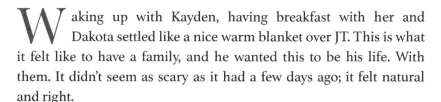

Waking up with Kayden, having breakfast with her and Dakota settled like a nice warm blanket over JT. This is what it felt like to have a family, and he wanted this to be his life. With them. It didn't seem as scary as it had a few days ago; it felt natural and right.

Kayden and Dakota were playing a color game in the Jeep as they drove to the hospital, pointing out the colors of motorcycles and cars, each having to find one of every color before arriving. He chuckled as he navigated a corner, turned into the parking lot and found a spot as close to the door as possible. He put the shifter in park, and said, "Done."

Dakota giggled. "I won, Mommy."

"That you did. You're very good at that game, Kota."

JT glanced at Kayden. "Ready?"

She nodded her head, but her expression told him she wasn't. He stepped from the Jeep and turned to open the back door for Dakota. "Come on, Red; let's go in and see Grandpa."

She laughed. "Why do you call me Red?"

He pointed to her little red boots. "Red."

She laughed again, the sound like music; it was so real and true.

Kayden held out her hand and Dakota slipped her tiny hand in her mom's and skipped along as they entered the hospital. Asking at the front desk for Oakes' room, they took the elevator to the fourth floor, then to room four eighty.

They were met in the hallway by Oakes' doctor, who was doing rounds and alerted that Kayden was on her way up.

He introduced himself as Dr. Tish and then pointed to a visitor's room just a door down. Once they had seated, he leaned forward, forearms on his knees.

"Oakes is extremely weak." He glanced at Dakota and then to Kayden. She nodded. "It's okay. She needs to know what to expect, too."

Dr. Tish looked at his hands, taking a moment it seemed to decide how to say what he needed for little ears.

"I will be surprised if he makes the night." Kayden sat back in the chair and swallowed several times.

"His heart is that weak?"

Dakota slipped from her chair and climbed into Kayden's lap.

"His heart has been weak for a long time, Kayden. He has congestive heart failure, and we've known this would happen sooner rather than later."

She softly cried into Dakota's hair, the little one whimpering into her momma's chest. JT swallowed as his heart broke for them. If it were his dad, he'd be devastated. He reached across and took her hand in his, feeling comforted himself when she squeezed him.

Composing herself, she sniffed, "He never said anything to me about his heart being bad."

Dr. Tish's expression was concerned. "I know, Kayden; he told me last night he never wanted you to know until he was gone."

She glanced at JT and he tried with his expression to let her know he was right here with her, for however long it would take.

Dr. Tish continued, "Under the circumstances, I think he's happy his time is up."

He glanced out the window that peered into the hallway to a door across the hall with two police officers standing post outside of the door.

"God, old man, what were you thinking?" she whispered. Looking at the doctor, she asked, "If he was this bad, how did he last so long while in the garage?"

Dr. Tish nodded his head. "He told me he faked the heart attack. At the time, he'd felt a twinge and hoped that the Devils would just leave them alone and not harm Dakota." He glanced at her little blonde curls, a soft smile on his face. "But, as time waned on, his heart rate increased as he heard Dakota crying. He said he tried to sit up and talk to her, but that's when he had his heart attack." Dr. Tish sat back in his chair. "I don't believe this particular heart attack was all that severe, but a heart in his weakened condition doesn't take much to cause damage."

She nodded and glanced at JT. He squeezed her hand and nodded to her.

"So, if I were you, I'd go in and say anything you need to say to him and know that he's been prepared for this for some time now." Dr. Tish looked each of them in the eye, glanced at Dakota and then asked if they had any questions. They shook their heads no and he stood to leave.

41

B racing herself for this visit, Kayden tried keeping her breathing even and steady as they walked to the door with the two police officers posted alongside. She looked at the taller officer, his striking blue eyes and friendly smile such a contrast to the starched uniform.

"May I ask why he's under guard?" She continued to hold Dakota's hand and JT's hand, too. She needed the comfort he offered to get through this. "I'm Kayden, Oakes' daughter."

"He's under arrest, ma'am. And we felt he might also need the protection."

Her lips straightened across her face and she nodded at him. "Thank you."

They had to show the officers their ID and submit to a pat down, which was fine with her, but when Dakota started crying because she was scared, Kayden got pissed all over again at what Oakes had put them through and it was only the beginning.

JT pushed open the door to Oakes' room and held it open for her and Dakota. As Dakota walked past him, he ruffled her hair and she smiled up at him.

A curtain separated the door and the bed to allow for some

privacy for the patient. Rounding the curtain, Oakes was lying completely still, the tubes and wires attaching him to the machines that were beeping, blipping and flashing numbers and lights on various monitors around the room. His left hand was handcuffed to the bed rail, the sheet and blanket covering him, completely smooth as if he hadn't moved since being covered.

Dakota froze as she peered around the curtain, and JT leaned down and picked her up. Kayden heard him whisper, "It's okay."

Stepping to the side of her father's bed, she glanced at the tube in his nose to help him breathe, and the ashen color of his skin. His breathing was shallow and the medicinal odor of the room made her feel a bit queasy. She placed her hand over his right hand. It felt cold and lifeless. Softly, she said, "Dad, Dakota, JT, and I are here to visit." JT stood on the other side of the bed, still holding Dakota in his arms. She softly cried into JT's shoulder; he calmed her by softly whispering words of comfort in her ear.

"Hey." His raspy voice sounded harsh in the room. His eyes landed on Kayden, then Dakota. Finally looking at JT, Oakes nodded and a crooked smile creased his face. "You take care of my girls, you hear me?"

"Yes, sir. You have my word."

Kayden turned to look in JT's eyes and was relieved to see he meant what he said. His posture stiffened as if speaking to a senior officer, his jaw tightened.

"Kota?" He sounded like he had marbles in his throat, but she picked her head from JT's shoulder and looked at her grandpa. "You mind JT and your momma and always be a good girl. I love you."

Dakota nodded her head. "I will. I love you, too, Grandpa."

Oakes closed his eyes a moment. His breathing labored.

After a few moments, he opened his eyes and trained them on Kayden. "I'm sorry, girl. I wanted to make some money to leave you two when I die. I never thought I'd get caught."

Tears sprang to Kayden's eyes. "Did you steal from the Devils?"

Taking a few breaths, he nodded slightly. "I took a small amount of marijuana from each package and sold it on my own. I wanted some hidden money. They got that during the robbery." He paused momentarily. "I had it in the hollowed out stock of my Mossberg."

"How'd they know that?"

"Rog. He knew that's where I hid things I felt were very important. It's the only way they'd know."

She glanced at JT and Dakota, who'd stopped crying and was intently listening. "Dad. Did you shoot Duncan?" Her voice cracked when she said it, the stupid tears threatening once again.

"No." Taking some deep breaths, he went on, "Idiots working for me did. I didn't tell them to." He looked into her eyes. "I'm sorry."

~

She softly cried, the tears flowing freely. She swiped at them as they fell, her head dipped low and her hair falling forward. JT listened quietly, not sure what—if anything—he should say.

"Kota, honey, give me a hug," Oakes said.

Dakota leaned forward and JT softly set her on the bed next to Oakes. She crawled up the side of the bed and laid down with her hand over his heart. The sight caused Kayden to cry harder. JT walked around the bed and pulled her into his arms, cradling her head on his shoulder and rubbing her back. He quietly rocked her back and forth, telling her it'd be all right.

The heart monitor beeped a solid beep, the line straight across the screen. Kayden raised her head and looked at her father's eyes, slightly open but not seeing. JT walked around the bed and pulled Dakota into his arms, returning to Kayden as nurses and Dr. Tish ran into the room, checking for a pulse or heartbeat. Dr. Tish spoke loudly over the voices, "He has a DNR order on file." The nurses continued checking monitors, one opened up a laptop and began typing quickly into her medical software. Once they did all they were allowed to do, Dr. Tish called the time of death at nine seventeen a.m.

Kayden and Dakota stood against the far wall with JT, watching the commotion and crying. JT's eyes welled with tears and he did his best to comfort his two women.

42

D r. Tish let them sit in the room with Oakes until the funeral home came to retrieve him. Kayden had never been in this situation before and she tried her best to explain things to Dakota. Dakota was a little girl with a thousand questions and when Kayden just couldn't answer any more of them, JT stepped right up and helped out. After the funeral home left with Oakes, JT called his dad and was told to bring them up to the house. The dinner they had planned to celebrate JT's big win was still on. The food had been purchased and after the shooting yesterday, no one was interested in going to Sturgis and felt like hanging out at the house. Since the bar would be closed, out of respect for Oakes, the house was the logical place for them all to be.

Entering the house around noon, the smell of cake baking in the oven wafted downstairs, and Dakota announced, "I smell cake."

Joci heard her exclamation and called down, "Come on up, Dakota; you can help us decorate cookies."

She ran to the stairs and made her way up as fast as her little legs could go. Kayden chuckled for the first time since the hospital. JT pulled her into his arms and kissed the top of her head. "I'm so sorry, baby. I'm here for you. You know that, right?"

She pulled back and looked into his sincere eyes. "I do know that and thank you."

Kayden pulled away and tucked her hands into the front pockets of her jeans. "I have to call my aunts about Dad. Do you mind if I use the bedroom?"

"Of course I don't mind. Do what you need to do. Let me know when you're ready to go to the funeral home to finalize arrangements. My mom and sisters will watch Dakota."

"Are you sure?"

He chuckled. "Hear the giggling up there?" They both trained their ears toward the kitchen at the top of the stairs. Dakota was laughing right along with the women as they decorated cookies and must have been making funny faces based on the conversation. "She'll be fine here, and I'll drive you so you can just relax and get your head around things."

"Okay. Thank you." She walked into the bedroom and closed the door, not sure who to call first. Her aunt Celia was Oakes' sister and the obvious first call. Her mom's sister, Joan, would be next, and then she'd need to call Payton and explain her father's part in Duncan being shot.

~

JT walked outside and bullshitted with the guys as they dragged wood that had fallen to the ground onto the platform built for firewood. They chopped it into manageable chunks and stacked it for later to build a fire.

After spending some time with Chase and Frog and his brothers, JT wandered to the upper deck of the house and leaned his shoulder against a post holding the roof over the deck. He watched the rock formation across the road where they'd seen the mountain lion the first night they were here. He'd love to see it before they left, but time was closing in on them now. If he looked down and to the left, he could see the guys setting up a game of bean bag toss and laughing. He wished his mood was as light.

Joci walked out of the front door and leaned on the railing next to him. "It sure is beautiful here, isn't it?"

Taking a deep breath, he nodded. "Yeah. It's gorgeous." He crossed his arms and continued to scan the hills.

Joci took a deep breath and slowly exhaled. "Are you staying, JT?"

His jaw tensed and released and he slowly flexed his shoulders. "I don't know, Mom."

She nodded her head. "Have you asked her to come back with you?"

He leaned on the rail next to her. "I offered it up as a suggestion that she could come and live with me."

She tucked fallen strands of hair behind her ear and looked at her hands folded in front of her, hanging over the rail. "Maybe you should ask."

He nodded. "Maybe."

43

The day flew by in a blur. They'd made a trip to the funeral home to make the funeral arrangements. A trip to the police station after they had called and had a few more questions. A trip to the hospital to visit Payton and Duncan. A trip home to grab some clothes for Dakota and herself because JT talked her into staying at the house so they could light off fireworks. Dakota could use the fun and distraction; the next few days would be difficult.

Descending the steps from her apartment, JT turned Kayden around to face him and pressed his lips to hers. She wrapped her arms around his neck and pulled herself up his body, wrapping her legs around his waist. He walked to the front of her Jeep and pressed her up against it. Her kiss became more insistent, her brain snapping on all cylinders as his scent enveloped her, his warmth and strength felt more like home than the home she was in right now. She pulled back and looked into his eyes, surprised at this thought and yet so confident and sure.

"The first time we made out was up against this Jeep. I've thought about it many times since then." His voice was gruff.

"I have, too." She was breathless with the realization that she wanted to be with him forever flooding her.

He unbuttoned and zipped her shorts and pulled them from her hips. Her panties followed closely behind. He lifted her onto the hood of the Jeep and looked into her eyes as he slowly spread her legs open. He smiled at her and it was devastating—her nerves were raw from the events of the past couple of days, but she needed him. He looked at her pussy and slowly circled his finger around the opening.

"I haven't properly tasted you, Kayden. Everything else about you is imprinted on my brain, but not your taste."

He leaned forward and licked her from bottom to top, swirling his tongue around her clit, then pulling it into his mouth, flicking his tongue over the sensitive bud. She moaned and pushed herself into him.

Reaching forward, she pulled the hair band from his hair and dug her hands into it. The thick lushness of it soothed her soul. He continued licking and sucking her until she moaned uncontrollably. He slid a finger into her channel and covered her with his mouth, drawing her in deeply until she quivered and exploded.

She laid back on the hood of her Jeep as JT continued to softly run his tongue into her wetness and swirling it around her clit. When her strength returned, she slowly sat up, and placed her hands on either side of his face, pulling him up to her. She kissed his moist lips, nipping and loving the feel of them against hers.

He grabbed her around the waist and pulled her from the hood, setting her feet on the garage floor. She immediately unbuttoned and unzipped his jeans and pushed them down his hips. He smiled at her and lifted her leg over his arm and pushed himself into her moist channel, seating himself fully inside her. The air whooshed from her lungs as she felt filled completely by him. Hearing his groans excited her. Her heartbeat increased and she felt light-headed.

He bent his knees and thrust up into her again and again, and she hung on to his shoulders, threw her head back and allowed herself to be consumed by him. His scent, his strength, his power—just him.

~

Driving back to the house, JT's cell phone buzzed. He pulled it from his back pocket and furrowed his brow. Tapping the answer icon, he said, "JT."

"Hi, JT. This is Richard from the Build-Off. I'm sorry I haven't called before now, we've been inundated with police interviews and the press hovering around trying to spin the story their way. Anyway, your bike will be released tomorrow from impound and I need to arrange a time to meet with you for pick up."

"Okay, I was actually going to call you and find out exactly that. What works for you?"

"Let's plan on eleven o'clock. And the news I'm sure you've been waiting for, JT. You are first runner-up, JT, and that's a fabulous honor. You'll be receiving a check from me for five thousand dollars and I'll give you that tomorrow."

Swallowing, he said, "Wow, that is an honor and thank you." He kept his voice even, trying to tamp down the disappointment.

"You deserve it and sorry again how it all worked out. See you tomorrow."

"Yeah. Thanks, Richard."

He tapped the end call icon and glanced at Kayden.

"Everything okay? That sounded like a good call."

He pulled the Jeep over to the side of the road. He leaned his forearm on the steering wheel and looked into her eyes. "I came in second, Kayd. The Build-Off. I didn't win."

She wrapped her arms around his neck and hugged him tightly. She peppered his face with kisses and the tears sped down her cheeks like a bike running the racetrack.

"Oh, JT, I'm so proud of you. Top three of all of those bikes. In the whole country. First runner-up is fabulous." She devoured his mouth, and held him as close as she could with a console between them. When she pulled away, she swiped at the tears and the smile she shined on him brightened his whole world.

He took her hands in his and kissed her fingers. "Thank you for making me feel better. I'm honestly honored. I'd just hoped for the top spot; you know?"

She smiled at him and softly said, "I know. But you have to admit that your first time, this is more than most would ever dream of."

44

E ntering the house hand in hand, it felt good walking into this house. Now they were all guests as the police would be confiscating this house as soon as the Sheppards left. They'd allowed them the privilege to stay just a few more nights.

The sadness and anger still inside were set aside to allow her to think of the future. Tomorrow would be time enough to grieve the father she thought she knew, not the drug dealer she'd been living with. She was determined to live without anger toward her father, though she knew it would take some time to get there. Disappointment wasn't a strong enough word for what she felt.

Joci called down the stairs, "Supper is almost ready; come on up when you can."

JT set the suitcase Kayden had thrown together into the bedroom and pulled her close and kissed her lips. "Let's go tell them about the Build-Off."

The closer they came to the top of the steps the louder the chatter became, Dakota's little voice right along with the others. She'd blended nicely with everyone. Entering the empty kitchen, they turned the corner to the dining room to see it filled with Sheppards, employees, and food. Dakota jumped out from behind Emma, a huge smile on her face. "I got new boots."

There she stood, bright smile on her face, yellow t-shirt, denim shorts and the cutest little biker boots she'd ever seen. "I match Molly and Emma now."

Kayden glanced at Dakota's new idols and saw they were wearing denim shorts and biker boots as well. She laughed and squatted down to hug the lively little bundle she loved more than her own life. "You look fantastic. Where did you get them?"

"We went shopping today." Dakota glanced back at Emma. "We tore it up." She giggled and glanced back at her new friends.

Kayden chuckled and looked at Emma and Molly. "Thank you for keeping her busy today and for her boots. I'm happy to pay you back for them."

Joci spoke up. "It was our pleasure, and my gift to Dakota." Leaning forward, she whispered, "Jeremiah hasn't seen the bill yet." The smile on her face was priceless.

JT cleared his throat. "We have an announcement."

The room grew quiet, expectations high. "I didn't win the Build-Off. I'm first runner-up."

Woots and clapping sounded around the room. Dog pulled JT in for a hug and said, "That's simply fantastic son. You've accomplished so much." His brothers and future sisters hugged and congratulated him as if he'd taken first place. At times when she let herself dream about a better life, this scene would pop in her head and she'd push it right back out, afraid to dream of something so good.

The evening passed and JT found himself smiling so much his cheeks actually hurt. As much as he'd dreamed of the Build-Off leading up to it, his family and Kayden had made him feel as if he'd won.

The dishes were cleared and they pulled blankets from the house and spread them out on the lawn to watch the fireworks display.

When the first one went off, Dakota clapped her hands and squealed in delight. Frog and Chase had been talking about their fireworks chutes for months. They'd been building them, practicing and perfecting them. This was their show and it was turning out to be a pretty damn good one at that. JT glanced over to see Dakota sitting in Kayden's lap, the smiles on both of their faces breathtaking. The colorful flashes of light illuminated their faces with colors, creating glowing effects on their cheeks and in their eyes.

This was the perfect culmination to the horrible beginning of today. He had been pissed at Oakes for his misdeeds, but he understood the passion and need behind it to make sure these beautiful ladies were taken care of. That would be his job now; but he'd do it with hard work and love.

45

Kayden finished pulling her hair up into a messy bun; the older black dress she'd pushed to the back of her closet would have to do for her dad's funeral. It still fit; that was a blessing. She slipped on her black pumps and left the bedroom in search of Dakota and JT.

The past two days had been both extremes—joyful and sad. The police found another cave on the property the big house sat on, and it was filled with bricks of marijuana. He'd been the mastermind behind the growing operation and they'd found stashes of cash all over the bar—in the ceiling tiles, the freezer, his apartment, the caves and in his motorhome. It was mind-boggling how he'd amassed so much money in a relatively short time. The police figured two years based on the information they'd gotten from some of the buyers they'd rounded up.

The big house the Sheppards were staying in and the five acres it was on were now the property of the federal government. The bar, fortunately, had been purchased years ago, so she just had to find a buyer for it. She'd work on that after the funeral.

She strode into the living room and found JT standing in front of the sofa, staring out the window at her dad's garage. He turned and whistled when he saw her. Giving her the once-over created tingling everywhere his eyes focused. He held out his arms to her and she willingly stepped into his embrace.

"You look beautiful, Angel." He breathed in her hair and she closed her eyes. "You always do."

She splayed her fingers across his back and thrilled at the definition of muscle under her fingers. The short sleeved black button up shirt he'd purchased in town for the funeral, while not his usual attire, was very sexy on him.

"You're a handsome man, Mr. Sheppard."

"I'm ready." Dakota walked into the living room, wearing a white cotton dress Kayden had purchased for her earlier in the summer and her black biker boots. She carried the red cowboy boots from her grandpa in her hand.

"What are you doing with those?" Kayden asked.

"I'm going to give them back to Grandpa. I'm a biker babe now."

Kayden kneeled down and looked into Dakota's sincere blue eyes. "Kota, you might want to wear them again, and Grandpa bought those for you."

She shrugged. "I know, but he bought them with drugger money and you had to give the house away because of that, so I should give my boots away."

JT swallowed and kneeled down next to them. "Kota, you don't have to do that. It's okay."

Dakota looked deep into JT's eyes. "It's okay. Every time I look at them now I think they're bad and I don't want to wear them anymore." Kayden was stunned at the maturity in the voice of such a small little gal.

Kayden looked into JT's eyes and saw the sadness in them that this little girl's favorite pair of boots were now tainted by the actions of her grandfather.

JT stood and took the boots from Dakota. "Okay, how about if I carry them for you?"

"Okay."

"I'd like to have a little talk."

He took Dakota's hand in his and said to her as he walked to the sofa, "I want to talk to you and your Mom about something."

She climbed up onto the sofa next to him, her little ankles crossed, and he chuckled. Looking up at Kayden, he held his hand out, beckoning her to him. She walked over and sat on the knee he patted, encircling his arm around her backside.

He looked into Kayden's eyes for a few seconds, admiring the greens and browns that blended so beautifully together.

"Kayden, I want us to start out a whole new life, together, the three of us. Will you marry me?"

She sucked in a breath and froze. She stared into his eyes, so long he almost squirmed. "Yes." It came out as a whisper.

"Really?"

"Yes. We'll marry you." She looked at Dakota, tears spilling from her eyes. "Won't we, Kota? Do you agree?"

The biggest smile that JT had ever seen graced her beautiful little face. "Do you mean you'd be my daddy?"

"Yes. I'd be your daddy. My mom and dad would be your grandma and grandpa for real. And if you wanted, I could adopt you and you could be Dakota Sheppard."

Her sparkling blue eyes sought Kayden's. "You want to marry JT, Mommy?"

"I do, very much."

Giggling, she said, "I want to marry JT, too."

Dakota lunged forward and wrapped her little arms around both of their necks.

JT hugged both of them for a long time and then set Dakota back on the sofa. "We have to make it official." He reached into his shirt pocket, his fingers slightly shaking, and pulled out a beautiful diamond halo ring with an oval diamond in the center. It was the most beautiful ring Kayden had ever seen in her life. Tears sprung to her eyes as he held her hand in his and asked, "Will you marry me, Angel?"

Swallowing profusely, all she could do was nod her head. He

slipped the ring on her finger and pulled her head down to kiss her lips.

He held up his index finger and then pulled a petite little gold chain from his pocket. He held it up to Dakota and showed her three little hearts in the middle of the chain. One in gold, one silver and one rose. "This is for you to seal the deal. Three hearts for three people in our family."

Dakota's mouth fell open, and in all of her five years, Kayden had never seen that little girl speechless, but she was now. JT ducked his head to look at her eye level. "Do you like it?"

She nodded, still stunned at the beautiful gift. "It's beautiful. I've never had my own necklace before. Momma said I was too little."

Kayden giggled and swiped at her tears. "I think you've grown up quite a bit these past few weeks."

JT motioned for Dakota to turn around and he placed the necklace around her neck. Though he struggled with the tiny clasp, he managed to get it together. Dakota turned around and touched the little hearts with her tiny fingers ever so lightly.

"Thank you, JT. I love it." She stood on the sofa and flung herself into their arms and hugged them tight.

〜

She let go, turned, and jumped from the sofa to the floor. "I have to go and look at it in the mirror."

She briskly walked from the room and Kayden giggled as she watched her little girl growing up before her eyes before turning to JT and kissing him deeply. Touching his face with her fingers and clasping the ponytail with her other hand, she slowly slid her tongue into his mouth, exploring it fully. He pulled her into his groin and she could feel his quickly growing erection against her thigh.

His voice raspy, he whispered, "Will you come home with me to Wisconsin?"

She pulled back and looked into his eyes. "There's nothing here for me anymore and honestly, earlier this week a feeling came over me and I just knew that my home is where you are. You're my home, JT."

He looked down at the ground and a small sob tore through his throat. He swiped at tears in his eyes and when his watery gaze met hers, he said, "You're my home, Kayd."

He kissed her lips fully, loving the feel of her lips against his. He reached up to lightly squeeze her breast.

She pulled away a fraction. "I'd love to celebrate with some hot monkey sex right now."

Chuckling, he said, "Me too."

Hearing little footsteps coming toward them, Kayden turned to see Dakota enter the room. She was adorable with her little blonde curls and her biker boots. "I was just thinking," she said as she walked toward them, "this means I can call you Dad."

JT's brows raised. "I guess it does. But only if you want to."

Dakota nodded. "I'll think about it."

They both burst out laughing, which caused Dakota to laugh with them.

The funeral was a big affair; everyone in the small town of Shady Pines came to pay respects to the man they'd known for the past fifty-seven years. Oakes had been born here and he died here, just like he'd always said he would. Kayden couldn't help but hear the whispers from some of the old biddies who insisted on making this about gossip and not paying respects, but she would be leaving this town soon enough. On the way to the funeral, they'd spoken to Dakota about staying in Shady Pines or going back to Wisconsin, and she wanted to go to Wisconsin where her new family lives.

Entering Grumpy's, the little restaurant on Main Street, after the funeral, JT and Kayden, holding Dakota's hands in theirs, found the tables set aside for their large clan. Payton, Ruby, and Chance joined them; Duncan had just been released from the hospital and for obvious reasons, wasn't interested in attending. Who could blame him? The Sheppards and their employees, Chase, Frog, Janice, and Ricky, who had been so supportive through all of the mess this past week. Her two aunts had come to the funeral, but declined to join them for dinner, citing a long drive as a reason. They both did come from a distance, but each were angry and embarrassed at the sham Oakes had been.

It was at the table after the food had been delivered that Dakota piped up and said, "Mom and JT are getting married."

Most of the group laughed and Ryder leaned forward and said to Dakota, "Did you catch them kissing again?"

She giggled. "No, silly. We told JT we'd marry him when he asked."

The table grew very quiet and all eyes turned to JT and Kayden. Kayden looked into JT's eyes and a smile grew upon her face. She slowly raised her hand to show off the rock he'd given her just a couple of hours ago and the mood turned to one of celebration.

Once the elation of the announcement died down, Joci looked over at the newly engaged couple and asked. "Will you be staying here or coming home?"

JT took Kayden's hand in his. "We're coming home."

Joci reached over and took JT's hand in hers and gave it a squeeze. "I'm so happy for you. Both of you."

Dakota said, "I'm getting married, too."

Joci chuckled and looked at Dakota. "I'm happy for the three of you. But Mommy and JT are getting married; you'll be part of it, but not getting married. You'll need to wait to meet your own Prince Charming and marry him."

Dakota cocked her head and looked at Joci. "I have to rescue him first."

JT and Kayden laughed and explained Dakota's meaning.

Jeremiah stood and held up his beer. "I'd like to make a toast." He nodded to the new couple, and said, "JT, Kayden, and Dakota, on behalf of everyone here, I'd like to congratulate you and welcome Kayden and Dakota into our family. Despite the disappointments we've had this week, I also want you to know that Oakes was a brother at arms and I loved him like one. I always will. Nothing he did diminishes that love. It's disappointing, but it doesn't erase all we were to each other."

He looked around the table and then down at Joci. She put her hand in his and he kissed her fingers before saying, "JT, when we get back home, I'd like you to head up our new design department. Your mom and I have been talking and with the new addition to the building, we have room to set up an office and a design center for you, Joey, and Chase to continue on with the great work you've done. If you accept."

JT looked into Kayden's eyes and the smile she bestowed on him said it all. He kissed her lips, stood and walked over to hug his dad. Pulling back, he said, "I accept."

Jeremiah held up his beer and waited for JT to pick up his. Raising it in the air, he said, "Cheers," to which the rest of the group repeated.

After the dishes had been cleared, Kayden stood to use the restroom. A man who had been sitting a few tables away, stood and intercepted her path. He held out his hand and introduced himself as Daniel Selisen.

"Your dad has spoken to me a number of times about buying the bar. I'm a miner and I mine mica."

He pulled his business card from his wallet and JT stood and walked over to see what the conversation was about. He handed JT another card and continued.

"I'd like to buy the property from you, Ms. Leathers. I'll pay you fairly; we can have it appraised and go from there."

Kayden turned to JT, the question in her eyes. "It's up to you, Kayd."

She nodded and turned to Daniel. "I'd like to explore selling the property to you. I'll see about getting an appraisal on the property and make sure you get a copy. Is that fair?"

He held out his hand and shook hers. "Yes ma'am, that's fair. Thank you."

46

The following morning, the Rolling Thunder group began packing to leave. As JT tossed the last of his clothing into his duffle bag, his phone rang. He picked it up from the nightstand and tapped the answer icon. "JT."

"Hello, JT, my name is Stu Baker. I'm the marketing director for Blaze Tires. I'd very much like the opportunity to sit down with you and discuss a licensing deal."

JT flopped onto the bed, staring out the window of the bedroom as the fluffy white clouds floated by.

Swallowing, he asked, "Licensing of what?"

"Sorry, I guess my intro wasn't that thorough. We noticed that you used our tires on your builder bike. We loved what you did with that bike. It's new, fresh and sexy. We'd like to talk to you about building some pilot bikes for us and our affiliates using our tires only and we'll use those bikes in all of our ads. They'll tour the country as we attend every major bike and car rally, race, show and whatnot. Your bikes can have your own signature logo on them, but they'll be licensed to us."

JT was speechless. Letting the news sink in, he swallowed the emotion beginning to rise to the surface. He broke out into a sweat, his heartbeat increased, and his hands shook.

"I hope I didn't lose you?"

Shaking the dismay from his head, JT quickly continued, "No. Sorry, I'm trying to get my head around what this means."

Stu laughed a hearty laugh from the other end of the phone and then added, "What it means is eighty thousand dollars a year. We're thinking we'd like six bikes next year and we'll talk after that about how we might want to expand. You can keep your job at Rolling Thunder; we know it's a family business. Just build us the set number of bikes each year and agree to pose for a few ads. We'll talk further about attending a few of our shows annually, but this can all be laid out in a contract."

JT coughed. That was a great sum of money. For doing something he loved? No-brainer. "I'll need to discuss this with my fiancée and my father. The four of us should sit down together. They're just packing up to leave Shady Pines in the morning. I'll be here for another couple of weeks."

"I'm still in Sturgis, let's get together this afternoon. Say, two-thirty?"

The bedroom door opened and Kayden strode in with a plate of food and a bottle of beer. She smiled as she walked around the bed and set his plate on the nightstand. His eyes never left her as he drank in her long legs and ample breasts, softly moving as she walked. Delicious.

"Sounds good. We can meet at Grumpy's in town. See you then." He pulled the phone from his ear and dropped it on the bed. Wrapping his hands around her hips, he pulled her down to him and slowly laid back with her on top of him. His hands gripped her ass and pulled her tight to him and his lips played over hers. She dug her hands into his hair and kissed his cheeks, then dipped lower and licked the rim on his ear. He groaned.

"Who were you talking to, JT?"

"An admirer."

"Hmm. You're not allowed to have those any more. Except me. I'm your only admirer now."

She kissed his neck and nipped at the tender skin; he took that moment to breathe in her hair and absorb the fresh clean scent of cotton and fresh air.

"Well, this one I think you'll like."

She slid to the side and laid facing him and he turned to face her. He told her about the phone call and she laughed. "This is so much better than winning the Build-off. Oh my God, JT, this is fantastic."

He laughed as he stared into her eyes, the happiness replacing the sadness that creeped in from time to time.

"I know." He chuckled again.

"Are you guys kissing again?" The sweet voice of Dakota broke into their mirth.

"Yes, we were kissing again," he said as he stood and pulled Kayden to her feet. "Let's go upstairs and find Grandpa, shall we? We've got some news."

~

Two weeks later...

JT closed the door on the trailer and locked it. He glanced back at the spot where the bar used to stand, but was now a pile of rubble. Daniel Selisen's wrecking equipment arrived early yesterday morning and made short work of the wooden building. He'd warned Kayden the day before to say her goodbyes, but only a couple of tears fell from her beautiful hazel eyes when the building fell over, and then she composed herself and slapped her hands together and exclaimed, "I'm ready for our new life, JT."

He hugged her close, and whispered, "I'm ready for our new life, too, Angel."

Dakota ran up to him, her pink backpack loaded with stuffed animals, books, and a little pink kids electronic reading device he'd purchased for her so she could fill it with hundreds of books and a few games for the road.

"I'm ready. Mommy's making snacks in the motor home."

He chuckled. They'd rented a nice motor home and a trailer for the trip to Wisconsin. The furniture she wanted to bring with them, her motorcycle, and their belongings were in the trailer. Frog and Janice were excited to drive her Jeep back home and took selfies with themselves in front of the Jeep at every state line.

JT helped Dakota carry her backpack up the steps into the motor home and set her down at the booth so she could eat. Kissing Kayden, he asked, "Almost ready?"

"Yep. I just wanted to make these little sandwiches and then we can hit the road." She stepped to the refrigerator and pulled out a bottle of water. She held it up to JT and he nodded. She handed it to him and took another one for herself. She poured Dakota some apple juice and said to JT, "Ready."

"Where are we going to live when we get there?" Dakota asked.

JT chuckled. "Well, I have a house that I just bought after Gunnar and Emma got engaged. We'll live there, but if it won't work for us, we'll sell it and buy a bigger one. Deal?"

She clapped her hands, and said, "Deal."

JT strapped himself into the driver's seat, Kayden sat in the passenger seat, and Dakota sat at the table, eating a snack and reading her books. They pulled out of the parking lot of the former OK Leathers Saloon and turned east. Kayden turned and watched out the side windows until Shady Pines had disappeared into the horizon. She was starting a whole new life with a wonderful man. It was more than she had ever let herself dream. She let out a deep breath and smiled at JT. "I'm going to love being your wife, JT."

He looked into her eyes. "'I'm going to spend the rest of my life making sure you do, Angel."

MOVING HOME, BOOK 6

Chapter One

"I 'll tell you this, Kayden Leathers. You owe the club a shit ton of money, and we aim to make sure we get it." The evilness in the face that stood in front of her made her heart hammer and her stomach twist tightly. The menacing hazel eyes and a scar running the length of the left side of his face and tight jaw screamed 'scary as hell.'

Mustering courage and working to keep her voice even, she replied, "I don't owe you or your club anything. Any deals you may have had with my father died with him." She moved to step around the club member in front of her, his tattoos proving his club affiliation with the Dakota Devils. He made to step in front of her.

"Everything okay here?"

Relief flooded her body when she heard Dan, the bank manager's voice behind her. The Devil in front of her shot Dan scowl and left the bank without a look back.

"Yes. Thank you, Dan. I can't wait to be far away from those guys."

"You'll do well to get out of town right away, Kayden; there are rumblings that they feel as though they've been screwed in some way and you're to blame."

Taking a cleansing breath, she worked to put a smile on her face. "I don't see how, but JT and Dakota are in the motor home waiting for me outside, then we'll be out of here. Thanks again."

Exiting the glass doors, she looked up and down the street, nervous about being accosted on her way to the vehicle. Relief swept through her when she saw no one lurking about. Hastening her steps to reach the motor home in the parking lot, she entered the side door as quietly as she could. When she'd gone into the bank, Dakota had been taking a nap, and JT agreed to stay with her while Kayden finished up her business here in South Dakota.

Directly across from the door were the dinette and table. Dakota still lay sleeping peacefully, her blonde curls in disarray, her ever-present biker boots still on her feet. The pink T-shirt with sparkling letters on the front captured the sun streaming in through the window above her. Her heart always swelled when she watched her daughter sleep.

Turning to lock the door, she moved to the front of the motor home where JT still sat in the driver's seat. Apparently, he was eager to get home. She knew he had a lot waiting for him there. They both did. She'd be lying if she didn't at least admit she was nervous, though not as nervous as staying here would be with the Devils still wanting money from her. Their anger swelled when they found out she'd sold the bar and property to someone else. They'd been so sure Oakes had changed his will to leave it to the club. Club members had swarmed the bar after they'd found out about the sale, yelling and swearing that they'd been robbed. Police had to come with a SWAT team to move club members away. They'd been so scared that they went to a neighboring town and stayed at a hotel until daylight when they could come back with police nearby and pack up as they had this morning.

"Everything okay?" JT's green eyes resembled fresh spring grass.

The stubble on his chin gave him that sexy bad-ass look, and his usual ponytail said 'biker' all the way.

"Yeah. How about out here?"

"She's been sleeping the whole time. Even snored a little bit, which I got on video." He chuckled as he scrolled through his phone. "Look at this."

He played the video of her daughter, slightly snoring and they both chuckled. "She's going to hate that video."

"I think its adorable. I sent it to Mom. By now, she's sent it to Molly and Emma, so it's out there."

Giggling, Kayden kissed his lips briefly. "We have to go, JT. One of the Devils stopped me in the bank still griping that I owe them money."

"Shit. I should have been in there."

"No, it was fine. But let's just go."

DEAR READER

Thank you so much for reading Moving Home. Did you know that when you rate a book with only stars and no text the author does not see it? It also doesn't help us with vendor ratings. But, by simply writing five words or more, this greatly helps us out so we can apply for promotions to further market our books. Would you please consider a few words along with your star rating? I thank you in advance and hope to see you on the internet.

Also, if you like to stay informed of all things related to my books, or love the chance to win a book from my author friends, join my reader's club, it's free and easy to do, just click on Readers Club below. Thank you.

PJ's Readers' Club

OTHER TITLES BY PJ FIALA

CONNECT WITH PJ

Reader's Club
PJ on Facebook
Tweet PJ
See inspiration photos on Pinterest
Goodreads

MEET PJ FIALA

Meet the Author

I was born in a suburb of St. Louis, Missouri named Bridgeton. During my time in Missouri, I explored the Ozarks, swam in the Mississippi River, and played kickball and endless games of hide-and-seek with the neighborhood kids. The summers spent in Kentucky with my grandmother, Ruth, are the fondest childhood memories for me.

At the age of thirteen, my family moved to Wisconsin to learn to farm. Yes, learn to farm! That was interesting. Taking city kids and throwing them on a farm with twenty-eight cows purchased from the Humane Society because they had been abused was interesting. I learned to milk cows, the ins and outs of breeding and feeding schedules, the never-ending haying in the summer and trying to stay warm in the winter. Our first winter in Wisconsin, one storm brought 36 inches of snow, and we were snowed in for three days! Needless to say, I didn't love Wisconsin.

I am now married with four children and four grandchildren. I have learned to love Wisconsin, though I still hate snow. Wisconsin and the United States are beautiful, and my husband and I travel around by motorcycle seeing new sites and meeting new people. It never ceases to amaze me how many people are interested in where we are going and what we have seen along the way. At every gas station, restaurant, and hotel, people come up to us and ask us about what we're doing, as well as offer advice on which roads in the area are better than others.

I come from a family of veterans. My grandfather, father, brother, two of my sons, and one daughter-in-law are all veterans. Needless to say, I am proud to be an American and proud of the service my amazing family has given.

Made in the USA
Monee, IL
30 August 2022

12847836R00125